TESTIFY

Also by Valerie Sherrard

Young Adult Novels
Kate
Sam's Light
Sarah's Legacy
Speechless
Three Million Acres of Flame
Watcher
Accomplice

Junior Novels
Tumbleweed Skies
The Glory Wind

The Shelby Belgarden Mysteries
Out of the Ashes
In Too Deep
Chasing Shadows
Hiding in Plain Sight
Eyes of a Stalker
Searching for Yesterday

Books for Younger People
There's A COW Under My Bed
There's A GOLDFISH In My Shoe

TESTIFY

VALERIE SHERRARD

DUNDURN
TORONTO

Editor: Shannon Whibbs
Design: Jennifer Scott
Printer: Webcom

Library and Archives Canada Cataloguing in Publication

Sherrard, Valerie
        Testify / Valerie Sherrard.

Issued also in an electronic format.
ISBN 978-1-55488-927-3

        I. Title.

PS8587.H3867T37 2011   jC813'.6   C2010-907299-5

1   2   3   4   5   15   14   13   12   11

Conseil des Arts   Canada Council   Canada   ONTARIO ARTS COUNCIL
du Canada   for the Arts   CONSEIL DES ARTS DE L'ONTARIO

We acknowledge the support of the **Canada Council for the Arts** and the **Ontario Arts Council** for our publishing program. We also acknowledge the financial support of the **Government of Canada** through the **Canada Book Fund** and **Livres Canada Books**, and the **Government of Ontario** through the **Ontario Book Publishing Tax Credit** and the **Ontario Media Development Corporation**.

Care has been taken to trace the ownership of copyright material used in this book. The author and the publisher welcome any information enabling them to rectify any references or credits in subsequent editions.

J. Kirk Howard, President

Printed and bound in Canada.
www.dundurn.com

Dundurn	Gazelle Book Services Limited	Dundurn
3 Church Street, Suite 500	White Cross Mills	2250 Military Road
Toronto, Ontario, Canada	High Town, Lancaster, England	Tonawanda, NY
M5E 1M2	LA1 4XS	U.S.A. 14150

CHAPTER ONE

This is it. This is the moment. All of the questions I've already answered have been leading to the one I know is coming next. My stomach clenches as I look out over the courtroom.

Being on the witness stand is scary.

The judge is to my right. He's younger than I thought he'd be — not much older than my father. I've glanced at him several times during my testimony and each time he has given me a small, encouraging nod. It's tempting to look toward him now, but I don't. I need to focus.

I take a long, deep breath to still the trembling inside me. My throat is dry, but I try to ignore that.

The prosecutor, Ms. Dewyn, has already talked to me about how I need to look when I answer. I've practised at home so it's easy now. I lift my chin and meet her eyes. She gives me a hint of a smile and continues.

"And what did you see when you entered the kitchen on that evening?"

"I saw Carrie and her stepfather, Joe Kelward. His back was to me, so he didn't know

I was there." This is so much harder than before, when we went over my testimony. Of course, the accused wasn't sitting a few feet away from me back then.

I fight to stay composed. I can't let panic cause me to fall apart on the witness stand. Too much is at stake.

"Take your time, Shana," Ms. Dewyn tells me. "You're doing fine."

"Then he reached out and touched her … breast with his right hand," I say. I don't mean to look at him, but I can't help it. He's staring at me hard. A shiver runs through me as I meet his dark, angry eyes, but then the trapped look on his face almost makes me want to smile. I want to tell him that this is what happens to creeps who touch young girls. They get caught and charged and sent to prison.

There are a few more questions from Ms. Dewyn before Kelward's lawyer, Mr. Hatton, gets up and cross-examines me. He wants to know if I'm sure of what I saw. He tries to shake me, to make me say I might have been mistaken. I don't budge. There's no way I'm going to let my best friend down.

And then it's over. My knees are shaking as I make my way past the table where Joe Kelward is sitting. This time I hold my head up and look straight ahead. I pass by without a glance in his direction. As the courtroom's big, wooden doors close behind me, I see Carrie, waiting on a bench in the hallway.

She leaps to her feet and rushes over to me. "How did it go?" she asks, grabbing my arm. Her face is pale and frightened.

"Okay," I say, and then she wants to know everything. I go over it all in as much detail as I can remember and watch as relief washes over her face. But we know it isn't over yet. It won't be over until the trial ends and the jury makes its decision.

Guilty or not guilty.

Carrie is trying not to think about what will happen if he's found not guilty. She says there's no way she could handle it if the jury was to set him free. I keep telling her that won't happen. It's easy to understand why she's nervous, though. She's been through so much.

The tap-tap-tap of heels clicking along the floor gets our attention. We turn to see Carrie's mom coming along the wide corridor. Her face is pinched and sad and I can't help but feel sorry for her. Six months ago she was newly married to what she thought was this super-great guy. It must have been awful for her to find out the truth, that her new husband was actually a child molester who had been after her own daughter.

Carrie throws her arms around her mom. Her mom hugs her back and says, "Hello, Shana," to me at the same time.

"Hi, Mrs. —" I hesitate, because I realize I have no idea what to call her now. I'd always known her as Mrs. Freeman, even after her divorce from Carrie's dad. Of course, when she remarried it was Mrs. Kelward, but I'm pretty sure she doesn't want to be called that anymore.

"I'll be going back to Freeman," she says, seeing my dilemma. "It seems simplest, especially since I hadn't had time to change things over before ... all of this happened."

"You'll be okay, Mom," Carrie says, touching her mother's arm. "So, do you think we could have money to go to Minato's for lunch? To say 'thanks' to Shana?"

"I don't need —" I say, but Carrie is giving me the "stop talking" look so I let it go. I feel guilty when her mom fumbles in her purse and passes over forty bucks.

"You know what? I'm not sure I'm in the mood for sushi after all. I think I'd rather just get a burger," Carrie says as we leave the courthouse. So, instead of heading west, we turn the other way to Barrington and make our way to the food court at the Maritime Mall. We order at Nick's Lunch and Carrie pays with one of the twenties.

Once we're settled at a table in the food court, Carrie leans forward, puts her hand on my arm and asks, "So, honestly, was it hard for you? Testifying?"

"Kind of," I say. Then I feel foolish. Carrie had been on the witness stand before me. She'd testified for almost two hours! And she was the victim.

"But I know it must have been so much harder for you," I tell her.

"It was pretty rough," she admitted, picking at the edge of the paper plate in front of her. "But it was worth it. I'll just be glad when the whole thing is over with."

My thoughts slip back to the day when Carrie found the courage to tell me what was going on. Her words had stunned me, but my shock turned to fury as I pictured Joe Kelward's smiling face. There he'd been, putting on a big act, pretending to be a nice guy, when all the time he'd been hiding a dark, evil side. Carrie was the only one who saw the truth all along. I remember her telling me right from the start that there was something about him she didn't like. She said that she didn't trust him and that he might be fooling everyone else, but he sure wasn't fooling *her*.

I wish I'd listened to what she was trying to tell me. Back then I just thought she was imagining things. I should have been a better friend. I hate that she had to go through that. More than anything, it kills me to know she kept her terrible secret for months before she finally broke her silence. She'd been feeling so trapped! No one had believed her when she tried to tell them the guy wasn't what he seemed — that inside, he was a monster. Why would she think anyone would believe her when that same monster started lurking in the corners of her life?

I remind myself that I came through when it mattered. The prosecutor said my testimony was really important because it backed up Carrie's story. She said that telling the jury what I saw would help get rid of any doubts they might have.

Which is all good except for one thing. I didn't really see anything. My whole testimony was a lie.

CHAPTER TWO

I know it's wrong to lie. Even worse than that, I know that lying in court is *really* serious. (I try not to think about the fact that it's called perjury and that it's actually a crime.) But before you judge me, there are two things you should know about why I did it.

The first one is that I would never have done something like this if there had been another way to help Carrie. And the second one is that I would do anything I could for her. She's the best and truest friend I've ever had.

We've gone to the same schools for ages, but we didn't get to be friends until three years ago. That's when we both got shipped off to the same summer camp. It was awful. Bugs and outdoor bathrooms and lousy food. On the second day there, Carrie cornered me and asked if I wanted in on a plan she was working on. I agreed even before I knew what the plan was. (You don't really need to know the embarrassing details. Let's just say it involved swimming — but it *didn't* involve bathing suits. Oh, and we got caught.)

It made us instant friends. By the end of the summer we'd upgraded to best friends and it's been that way ever since.

Carrie was the one who got me through the breakup with Mike Rebonair last fall. He was the first guy I'd gone out with that I really, really liked. A lot. It lasted for three and a half months — from August third to November nineteenth. It was a new and thrilling kind of happiness for me and I thought he felt the same way. Except that, one day, just like that, I found myself dumped. It was the cruellest, lowest way he could have done it, too — by changing his relationship status on Facebook. I never even knew why! He'd been at my place just an hour or so before that and I'd thought everything was fine.

Carrie was there when I found out. In fact, she was the one who noticed it when she used my laptop. I sat on my bed bawling my head off while she tried to cheer me up by changing *my* status as well, and then posting nasty things about him on my Facebook account. It didn't help. For a while, nothing did. I was devastated.

That was why, for weeks afterward, Carrie would show up at my place and make me let her in even if I said I wanted to be alone. One time she came over with a full container of brownie-batter ice cream and refused to leave until it was all gone. She said it was impossible to eat that much chocolate and stay sad. She was right. By the time we'd gotten through it, we were giggling and I felt a little better.

This summer Carrie came up with the idea of sharing a babysitting job for Mrs. Hauser down the street. Her usual sitter only watches kids after school, so she needs someone when school is out. I wasn't keen at first. I like kids okay, but who wants to spend their whole summer babysitting? Carrie's idea of splitting it up was perfect. She pointed out that it was the only job we could get where we'd have every weekend off. Besides that, we could divide the time however we wanted. Most weeks we split it up — two or three days each, so it hardly felt like we were working at all.

The money wasn't bad, either. Mrs. Hauser paid fifty bucks a day, so it worked out to a hundred and twenty-five dollars a week each. We always divided the money evenly, even though I actually ended up working nine days more than Carrie by the end of the summer. I didn't want to make a big deal over it, so I never said anything to her about that. After all, it had been Carrie's idea in the first place, and she was the one who talked Mrs. Hauser into hiring us.

Just like the job, we do almost everything together. Movies, dances, shopping — everything is more fun with Carrie. If there's anything going on, she's right there in the middle. And if there's nothing going on, she dreams something up. For example, she organized a flash mob down by the harbour one Saturday afternoon. There were about thirty of us, and when she gave the signal, we all pointed to the sky and went, "Ooooo!" It was hilarious! Everyone around us was straining to see what was up there. Of course, there was nothing. It's impossible to be bored with Carrie around.

But it's more than that. Carrie is one hundred percent loyal. I know she would stand up for me anytime to anyone. You don't find friends like that every day.

So, you can see how it was. I know that lying in court was wrong. But my friend was in trouble and she needed my help desperately. I wasn't about to let her down.

I couldn't.

Carrie wants me to sleep over at her place that night after court. It's a school night, but Mom says I can. She says she understands my friend needs support right now. There's a shadow in Mom's voice lately. She and my dad were really shaken by what happened to Carrie. And it scared them to think that Joe could have tried something with me, too. It took a while to calm them down and reassure them that he never touched me.

Carrie is nervous about what the jury will decide.

"What if they believe *him*?" she asks over and over. "What if they let him go?"

"They won't," I promise, but I'm worried, too. I keep seeing his face, and the way his eyes burned through me when I was on the stand. It's scary to think about what he might do if the jury sets him free.

The worst thing is that juries *do* make mistakes. Anyone who lives in my house would know that. My mom is totally addicted to true crime. Books, television shows, movies — it doesn't matter. If it's about a crime, she'll read it or watch it. And if she can corner me, she tells me all about it afterward.

When she finishes giving me all the details, she always says the same thing: "You never know what a jury will do!" Most of the time she agrees with their verdict. But not all the time.

Mom gets totally outraged when someone she believes was guilty is found innocent. Other times she's just as upset about a guilty verdict. That doesn't happen as often. And it's not necessarily because she thinks the person is innocent. Usually, she just doesn't think there was enough proof for a conviction. Reasonable doubt and all that. Mom takes her responsibilities as a crime fan very seriously.

It's interesting sometimes. But I never once thought a jury's decision would matter that much to me. Or to my best friend.

CHAPTER THREE

Closing arguments are the next day. I'm supposed to be at school, but I figure I'll deal with that later. It's more important for me to be here with Carrie. Her mom is there too, of course. She thinks my folks gave me permission to miss school.

When the prosecutor gets up and goes over the case, I start to feel better. She's so convincing, I'm sure the jury will find him guilty.

But then the defence lawyer has his turn. And suddenly, it doesn't look like such a sure thing. The lawyer talks about how Joe Kelward has no criminal record. Then he makes a big deal out of the fact that there is no physical evidence against his client. Next, he reminds them of what the character witnesses said. They were people who had known Joe for years. And they all said Joe is a good and decent man, that he is someone they trust. He tells the jury that an innocent man's fate is in their hands. The last thing he says is that they need to do the right thing and find Joe Kelward not guilty.

Carrie is pale and trembling beside me. As the jury files out she slumps forward. I see her wipe away the tears that have begun to fall. Her mother slides an arm around her and tells her not to worry and that everything will be all right.

I glance at Mrs. Freeman's face. Her eyes are brimming with sorrow. It makes me so angry, to see Carrie sobbing and her mother so full of grief. How could someone do what Joe Kelward did? How could he not care about the horror he was causing? Carrie's mom loved and trusted him. How could he have betrayed her and her daughter so completely?

I shake off these thoughts as we stand and make our way out of the courtroom and along the wide hallways to the door. The prosecutor has promised to call Mrs. Freeman as soon as the jury comes back with a verdict. She also warned us that it might not be today.

Carrie begs me to ask my folks if I can stay at her place again that night. I'm doubtful they'll agree, but willing to give it a try. Mom is most likely to let me, so I look for her first when I get home. I find her in the kitchen chopping celery for a cold pasta salad she's making. She's humming while she works. Until she sees me, that is. Then she puts the knife down very deliberately. She stands up, crossing her arms in front of her. Her face does not look happy.

"Would you care to tell me where you were today?" she asks.

Uh-oh. The school must have called home. I'd been hoping that wouldn't happen — their reporting system is kind of hit and miss. Now, not only is it out of the question that I'll be allowed to sleep at Carrie's place again, but it's guaranteed that I'll get grounded. "I went to court with Carrie," I admit.

"Without asking?"

That seems like a pretty dumb question. It's obvious that I did it without asking. I hang my head and try to look contrite. Mom doesn't buy it.

"You know, Shana, your father and I *try* to treat you like a responsible young adult," she says. It's the beginning of a lecture I've heard a hundred times. I tune her out, and think about some songs I want to put on my iPod. When the lecture is over I go to my room and call Carrie with the bad news.

"I got busted for ditching school," I tell her. "So now I'm grounded for a week."

"Maybe you could sneak out and come over, anyway. Just for a little while," she says.

I think about it for a few seconds. It wouldn't be the first time I've crawled out my window. Not when I've been grounded, though.

"I can't," I tell her. "If I get caught I'll be killed."

"Well, okay," Carrie says with a sigh. "I'll see

what Krysti is doing. I just need *someone* here!"

Krysti Walton is one of the girls in our circle of friends. I'm surprised that Carrie is calling her, instead of Jen or Hayley or Lori. After all, Krysti is the newest one in the group. She just moved to Halifax a few months ago. I forget exactly how she got to be part of the group, but she's definitely one of us now. Not that I don't like her — I do. I'm just surprised at Carrie's choice.

"Sorry you got in trouble," she tells me. "But I'm glad you were there."

"So am I. And I wish I could be there again tomorrow, but there's no way," I say. "Are you coming to school afterward?"

"Maybe. It depends what time the jury comes back with a verdict," Carrie says.

There doesn't seem to be much else to say then. I let her go and flip open my laptop to check my Facebook. That leads to some YouTube videos and then a couple of clips on Vimeo.

A while later Dad taps on my door. He tells me it would be nice if I gave my mother a hand with dinner once in a while. It sounds like a suggestion, but I know better. I head to the kitchen.

CHAPTER FOUR

The next morning drags by at school. I check for text messages between every class, but there's no news.

My stomach is actually hurting by lunchtime. Hayley, Jen, and Krysti are at our usual table when I get to the cafeteria. I grab today's combo — a salad with a slice of vegetarian pizza — and join them.

"I'm going nuts waiting to hear from Carrie," Krysti says. "Has she texted you yet, Shana?"

"Not yet," I say. I have to admit, I'm just a bit relieved that she hasn't sent anyone else a message, either. Not that I really thought she would.

"What's taking them so long?" Jen wonders out loud.

I wish she hadn't said that. I've spent the morning trying to remember which side it's usually good for when the jury takes a long time to reach a verdict.

It looks like Hayley is worried, too. She's silent, and her face is grim as she bites into her sandwich. I look down at the lunch I just bought. I pick up my fork and spear a tiny tomato from my salad, but it doesn't quite make it to my mouth. I'm not sure if eating will help, or make me feel worse. I'm staring at the food on my tray, trying to make up my mind, when all of a sudden Carrie appears beside us.

There's a huge smile on her face.

"They found him guilty," she says as she hugs me. While she's hugging me she whispers, "Thank you so much, Shana! I couldn't have made it through this without your help."

Relief rushes through me. I hug her back, but my throat is too tight to speak. It's over. It's really over.

"He got three years," she tell us. "Not long enough if you ask me, but by the time he gets out of prison I'll have graduated and moved on. I'll make sure he can't find me."

It hadn't occurred to me that Carrie might be worried that Kelward would come after her some day. I wonder if she's counting on him serving his whole sentence. From the things I've heard from my crime-fan mother, I know that isn't likely.

"He probably won't show his face around here again, anyway," I say. I decide not to mention that he could be out in a year or so, if he keeps out of trouble in prison. There's no point in her worrying about something that might not happen.

"So, good. That's over with," Hayley says. She looks down at the table as she speaks. "Can we just drop it now? It feels like this is all we've talked about for months."

A strange feeling runs through me. There's something wrong about Hayley's reaction. Carrie must think so, too, because I see a flash of anger in her eyes. I can't blame her for that. She needs her friends' support right now, and Hayley's comment wasn't exactly sympathetic.

What bothers me right away is the fact that it's not like Hayley to be uncaring. She's *always* the first one to help out when anyone in the group has a problem.

Hayley glances up and around the table. She sees that we're all looking at her. Almost at once, her eyes drop back. For a few long seconds she stares at the rest of the sandwich in her hand. Then she leans forward and takes a tiny nibble. She chews it slowly, like she's a judge at a taste contest of some sort.

I'm searching my brain for something to say — anything that will ease the sudden tension at the table. But I'm not fast enough. The next thing I know, Carrie is on her feet. Her eyes are brimming with tears. She looks like she's about to speak, but then she turns and hurries away instead.

"I'll go," Krysti says to me as I start to get up. "You haven't eaten your lunch yet."

To be honest, I'm too stunned by what has just happened to know what to say to Carrie, anyway. It's a relief to let Krysti go after her while I try to sort out the jumble of thoughts that are racing through my head.

Hayley lifts her eyes again. There's a haunted look on her face. It's like she's pleading with me to understand and not be angry with her.

"What's going on?" I ask as gently as I can.

She shakes her head.

A suspicion is growing in me. Is it possible that Hayley has *also* been a victim of sexual abuse? Why else would she be so uncomfortable with the subject? Maybe something happened to her in the past and she's pushed it down. Or maybe something is happening in her life right now — something she can't bring herself to talk about.

I swallow hard. I want to ask her, but I'm not sure what to say. If she's uneasy talking about it, saying the wrong thing might make it worse. And what if I'm wrong and I just embarrass her for nothing?

Finally, I find some words. "I don't know what just happened here, Hayley, but it makes me think something is wrong. If there's ever anything you want to talk about, I hope you know I'm here for you. Anytime."

Hayley's mouth opens and closes a few times. She clears her throat and glances around nervously.

"Thanks, Shana," she whispers. "But I don't know who I can trust."

Once again, I have no idea what to say. We pick at our food in silence for the next few minutes and then Hayley says she needs something from her locker and leaves.

I want to talk to Carrie before classes start, but when I find Krysti a bit later she tells me Carrie went home.

"She's so hurt by the way Hayley treated her," Krysti says. "She had been planning to stay this afternoon, but after that she just couldn't face anything else."

"Carrie isn't usually that sensitive," I say. "I'm sure it's just all the emotion of the whole court thing and having to tell strangers what happened to her."

"Probably," Krysti agrees. "But it wasn't very nice of Hayley to talk to her like that, either."

I say nothing to that. I want to defend Hayley, but that would feel like betraying Carrie. And, in any case, I have no proof of why Hayley acted the way she did.

What I mostly want is for everything to be back to normal. It bothers me any time there's conflict in the group. I've always been the type to try to keep peace. If something needs to be smoothed over, I'm right there.

And, of course, since I'm grounded, I can't

go to Carrie's after school. I try Skyping her when I get home, but there's no answer on her computer. She also hasn't answered the two text messages I sent between afternoon classes. It's not until later in the evening that I finally get a call from her.

"We need to do something fun!" she says as soon as I've answered. Her voice is happy and excited. "Let's have a party this weekend!"

"I'm grounded," I remind her.

"Yeah, but your mom usually lets you have friends over even if you're not allowed out," she says.

"True. But she's not about to let me have a party."

Carrie giggles. "That's the fun part. What if we do it on the sly? Like, a secret party going on without your mom or dad even realizing it's happening?"

I have my doubts that a crazy idea like that will work, but I can't help getting caught up in her enthusiasm.

"And just who would come to this secret party?" I ask. I can picture one of those out-of-control scenes with a guest list that reads like *Who's Who? As in, Seriously, Who ARE these People?*

"That's why it will work!" she says. "It will just be the six of us — you, me, Krysti, Jen, Hayley, and Lori."

I'm super relieved to hear Carrie include Hayley. That must mean she has decided not to make a big deal over what happened at lunch. I listen with increasing interest as she outlines her plan for the party on the weekend. She suggests that we do it in the afternoon. We can do make-overs and then just hang out. It's not as great as most of her ideas, but it sounds better than kicking around the house by myself!

CHAPTER FIVE

Saturday rolls around and I spend the morning helping Mom out with some chores. I try to keep it from being obvious that I'm trying to get on her good side. It makes her nervous when she gets the idea that I'm up to something. That happens quite easily, what, with all of the exposure she's had to true crime. Not to mention her suspicious nature. And the fact that this isn't the first time I've tried to do something sneaky behind her back.

My dad is so much easier. You could practically shout, "We're having a secret party here later," right in front of him and there's still a pretty good chance that it wouldn't register in his brain.

The girls arrive one at a time. Carrie is first and she comes in through the back door like she owns the place. I hear her chatting with my dad. He's not saying much, and I find out why when I get there. Dad is standing in front of the open fridge. He's eating cold meatballs out of some leftover spaghetti.

"Here comes Mom," I tell him in a loud whisper.

Dad slaps the lid on the container and shoves it back into the fridge. He turns, ready to face the music, but smiles when he realizes Mom is nowhere in sight. "You got me," he says, reaching for the dish again.

"Your dad is so nice," Carrie says after he's left the room. Her face is sad and I know she's probably thinking about her own dad. She hoped her parents would get back together for a long time after they split up. I guess that's common, but I don't think it happens very often. And the strange thing is, Carrie was always telling me how terrible things were before the divorce. Doors slamming, yelling, meals eaten in tense silence. Why would you want that back?

Then her mom got remarried, and you know what happened after that. No wonder she feels sad when she sees her friends' dads. Not that we all have our fathers at home. In our group, Jen and I do, but Krysti's and Lori's parents are also divorced. Hayley's parents and an older brother died in a boating accident when she was three. She lives with her grandparents. So, Carrie isn't the only one who doesn't have two parents at home.

I'm distracted from these thoughts by the sound of knocking at the door. It's Jen. She's barely inside when I see Krysti heading toward the house. Lori and Hayley arrive about ten minutes apart over the next half-hour.

Now that everyone is here, we head to my room. It's a bit crowded, but Carrie wants to show us a couple of YouTube clips. I've suggested taking my laptop downstairs to the TV room, but Carrie thinks that's a bad idea.

"We'd have to be careful about what we watched in case your mom or dad came along," she points out. "Remember that time your mom totally freaked over that video of that kid who broke his collarbone?"

"That was *so* gross," Jen says. She turns to Krysti, who wasn't yet part of the group back then. "The bone was sticking right out of his neck."

Krysti makes a suitably disgusted face. It reminds me of how my mom looked when she walked into the room and saw what we were watching. She didn't exactly freak, as Carrie put it, but she launched into a big lecture about the things we were filling our heads with. I have to admit that it was pretty annoying. Not to mention embarrassing.

So, we watch videos for a while. Each of us remembers something we've seen lately that we want to show the others. We're laughing over a cat playing piano when Mom taps on my door. I open it expecting her to be angry, but she surprises me.

"You can't be very comfortable, all squashed in here," she says.

"It's a bit crowded," I admit.

"Well, if you're interested, I've put out some snacks downstairs," Mom tells me. She arches an eyebrow and adds, "After all, you can't have a party without something to munch on."

My mouth is still open as she smiles, turns, and disappears down the hall and around the corner. I've stopped asking how she knows things at times like this. When I do, she tries to look mysterious and says she'll never tell.

We head down to the TV room where Mom has put out a bowls of pretzels and popcorn, some veggies and dip, and a herbed cheese ball with crackers. She's also made a pitcher of iced tea.

"When *I* get grounded, I have extra chores," Jen grumbles. "Shana gets to have friends over and her mom makes a buffet of snacks for them."

"Yeah, she sure has it rough," Lori says, smiling.

I'm about to answer when my eye is caught by the sight of Carrie wiping her eyes. Her head is down and I can see that she's trying to hide tears from the rest of us. Krysti has noticed too. She hurries to Carrie's side and slips an arm around her shoulders.

"You've been through some rough things," Krysti says quietly, "but it's all over now. You're safe."

Carrie's head comes up slowly. Her eyes are still wet and sad, but a smile trembles on her mouth as she looks around at each of us. She hugs Krysti and then moves to her left, hugging Jen and Lori and me. She reaches Hayley last, but once again, something isn't right. Hayley stands stiff and stone-faced. She doesn't react as Carrie hugs her and then turns to speak to all of us.

"I couldn't have made it through without you guys," she says. She pauses and glances doubtfully at Hayley before adding, "I have the best friends in the world."

It was a warm, sweet moment.

And then everything turned ugly.

CHAPTER SIX

"*Poor* Carrie," Hayley says. Her voice is thick with sarcasm.

We all turn at the same time. We stare in shock, hardly able to believe what we've just heard.

"Seriously, am I the only one getting tired of the drama?"

"The *drama*?" Krysti echoes. "Is that what you call it, Hayley?"

"Wait," Carrie says suddenly. "I think I know what's going on here."

There are a few seconds of silence and then she takes a deep breath. In a few quick steps she's moved over to Hayley. Carrie's hand reaches up and touches Hayley's arm ever so gently. Her voice is soft and caring as she says, "I think something else is bothering Hayley. And it's okay, Hayley. You're with friends. We'll do our best to understand and support you if you just open up and tell us."

It looks like Carrie has figured out what I suspected. I'm hardly breathing as I wait to see what will happen next.

"Look, Carrie, I don't know what you're trying to —" Hayley begins.

"I'm trying to help you, Hayley. I know about your problem. I've known for a while, but I haven't wanted to say anything to the others."

"*What* problem?" Lori blurts.

"Stealing," Carrie says.

"*Stealing*?" I repeat before I can stop myself. Not quite what I was expecting. "What are you talking about, Carrie?"

"I noticed a few of my things had gone missing after Hayley was over," Carrie said. Her voice is sad and low; her eyes are downcast. "I didn't want to believe it at first, but I started watching her. Today, I caught her in the act."

"You LIAR!" Hayley shouts. Her face is flushed and furious.

"Am I?" Carrie asks gently. "Then I didn't see you taking something from Shana's jewellery box a little while ago?"

"That's ridiculous," Hayley snaps. "I've never stolen anything in my life."

"Stop!" Lori says. She swallows hard. "I've had some things disappear, too. Including the sapphire ring my dad gave me last September — for my birthday. It disappeared about a month ago."

"I don't know anything about your ring, or anything else," Hayley insists. She's looking

34

around at us. I can tell that she's hoping to see signs that someone is on her side, but we're all too stunned to react.

"Well, it should be easy enough to prove," Jen says, finally breaking the silence. "Carrie says she saw you take something today. So, just turn your pockets inside out and empty your bag. If she's made a mistake, we'll soon know it."

"Not necessarily. She might be smart enough to have hidden whatever she took," Carrie points out. "That would protect her from getting caught. It could be anywhere in the house. All she'd have to do is get it before she leaves."

"What a convenient theory," Hayley snaps. She's furious, and already tugging at her pockets to show us they're empty. When she finishes, she opens her bag and turns it upside down on the end table. There's lots of stuff in there: a change purse and wallet, lip balm, hand cream, theatre stubs, two packages of gum, a folding hairbrush, and a few other odds and ends. But no jewellery of any kind. Nothing at all of mine.

"See!" Hayley says. Her teeth are clenched.

"What about the cellphone pocket?" Lori asks.

Hayley sighs and rolls her eyes. She tugs at the Velcro flap and pulls out her phone. Setting that aside, she turns her bag upside down once again.

We all see something fall to the carpet. We all step closer to get a better look. I'm the only one who can identify it, though, and that's because it's mine. An antique brooch that once belonged to my great-grandmother has just dropped out of the cellphone compartment on the side of Hayley's purse. I feel like I might be sick.

"I did *not* take that!" Hayley says. She turns to face Carrie. "You put it there! You set me up."

Carrie shakes her head sadly. "Hayley, we don't want to judge you. Whatever is making you do this — let us help."

Hayley's fists are clenching and unclenching at her side. I'm scared she's actually going to haul off and hit Carrie so I step between them. Hayley's eyes meet mine.

"I would never take anything from you, Shana," she says. "I would never take anything from *any* of you. I'm not a thief."

Hayley looks around at us. Her face pleads with us to believe her.

"Admitting that you have a problem is the first step," Carrie says softly.

"The only problem I have is *you*, you lying —"

"Carrie?" Krysti says, interrupting. "Just out of curiosity, why didn't you say something before now if you've known about it for months?"

"I didn't want to embarrass Hayley," Carrie says. "I'd been hoping that she'd come to her senses and put back the stuff she took. But when I saw her stealing again today, I realized that isn't going to happen. She probably needs professional help."

"That ring my dad gave me was really important to me," Lori says. She looks at Hayley with sad, pleading eyes.

Hayley barely glances at Lori. She's too busy stuffing things back into her bag. She throws it over her shoulder and clears her throat. "Do all of you actually believe I've been stealing from you?" she asks.

The room goes completely silent.

"I guess that answers my question," Hayley says. Then she walks out.

CHAPTER SEVEN

No one speaks for a few moments. The first sound comes from Carrie, who has begun to cry. Krysti is closest to her. Once again she puts an arm around Carrie's shoulders and tells her it's okay.

Of course, she's wrong.

It's definitely not okay.

"I shouldn't have said anything," Carrie sobs. "Now Hayley hates all of us."

"I don't think she *hates* us," I say. "She's just upset right now."

"I handled it all wrong," Carrie says miserably. "I should have spoken to her in private when I first realized she was stealing. It must have been humiliating for her to get caught red-handed that way."

"Don't you think *we* should be the ones who are upset with *her*?" Lori asks. She looks down at her hand, like her missing ring might magically appear there. "After all, it's our stuff she's been stealing."

"If she's been taking things, there must be some reason behind it," I say. "She needs her friends more than ever."

"I doubt that she still considers us her friends," Carrie says. "Not with her stealing out in the open. She probably sees us as enemies now. It's so sad."

"One of us should go and talk to her," Jen suggests.

"I'll do it," Carrie tells us. "I was actually just about to say that I'd go and talk to her."

"I don't think that's the best idea," Krysti says. "She's really furious with you. I think it would be better if someone else went."

"It's *because* she's angriest at me that I should go," Carrie says. "She'll know for sure that we all care, if the person she attacked the most still wants to work things out. I'll just give her a day or two to cool off and then I'll talk to her."

I wasn't sold on the idea. And by the looks on the others' faces, they weren't, either. But none of us wanted to argue about it. There'd been enough arguing for one day. So, we reluctantly agreed, and then tried to get back to having fun.

That didn't work. It's hard to force yourself into having a good time when something is troubling you. I found myself going over and over what had happened. Again and again I saw Hayley lift her purse up and shake it. I saw the brooch fall and I saw the shocked look on her face. That troubled me. Why would she be shocked if she knew it was in there?

I mention this to Jen later, when the two of us have gone to the kitchen to make more iced tea.

"Maybe she thought it wouldn't fall out. Like, if she had it pinned in there or something, but it came loose," Jen says. Her eyes narrow a little. "Or maybe she thought she could convince us she was innocent if she acted shocked."

I think about that while I stir the pitcher of powdered mix, water, and ice cubes. By the time I toss in some lemon slices I'm pretty much convinced that Jen is right. If Hayley knew she was caught and there was no way out, pretending to be horrified when she saw the ring might have been her only option.

"You saw how she tried to say Carrie set her up," Jen adds. "That was ridiculous. And remember it was right after Carrie said if we didn't find anything on her, then Hayley might have hidden it in the house somewhere? Why would Carrie have said that if she knew it was in Hayley's bag?"

"True," I say. "Anyway, Carrie would never do anything like that."

"Of course not," Jen agrees. "Why *would* she?"

"Exactly," I say. And the idea is ridiculous. Hayley *must* have taken the brooch. The only other possible explanation is that Carrie really did set her up and that's out of the question.

For starters, there's no motive. If there's one thing I've learned from listening to my mom talk about crime, it's that there is *always* a motive. She likes to corner me now and then and rhyme this stuff off like she's a giving a seminar at a legal conference.

"You need to do more than just look at the evidence," she'll say after giving me a quick rundown on the latest crime that's crossed her path. "You've got to ask yourself, who had a motive, and what was it? Greed? Jealousy? Anger? Revenge? Sometimes someone commits a crime to cover up another crime. Sometimes it's for some kind of emotional payoff. And every now and then it's hard to figure out why someone did something. But there's got to be a reason — even if it only makes sense to the person committing the crime."

And what motive could there possibly be for Carrie to do something like that to Hayley?

I think back to the way Hayley acted at school the other day. I'm wondering if that could have upset Carrie more than I realized, when it hits me.

The thefts have been going on for at least a month! That's when Lori's ring went missing. So something that happened this week couldn't have anything to do with it.

It's disappointing to think of Hayley as a

thief. But it would be even worse to think of Carrie as someone who would betray a friend in such a terrible way.

CHAPTER EIGHT

I can't stop turning this all over in my head. I get hardly any sleep on Saturday night. Sunday drags along while I think about one idea after another. By the evening, I have pains in my stomach. I decide to send Hayley a message. Except I can't.

It takes a few minutes before I realize that the problem I'm having isn't because of any kind of Facebook glitch. I've been unfriended. A quick check shows me that I'm not alone. Hayley is no longer on any of our friend lists. She's even gone so far as to block us — or me, at least.

I send Carrie a frantic text message. Mainly, I want to know if she talked to Hayley yet. She answers that she did, but it went worse than she expected. A lot worse. She says she's busy, but she'll fill us all in at lunch tomorrow.

Hayley is at her locker when I get to school in the morning. She turns away as soon as she notices me. A moment later, she breezes by with her books. Not a word, not a glance. It's like we're complete strangers.

But that's the point, isn't it? That I really don't know her. If you'd told me a week ago that Hayley was stealing from her own friends, I wouldn't have believed it. And now she clearly wants nothing to do with any of us.

At noon, Carrie looks grim when she fills us in on what happened. We sit listening with our lunches hardly touched.

"I just showed up at Hayley's place," she begins. "I figured that was the best thing to do. I didn't want to give her a chance to tell me not to come."

Krysti nods. "That was probably a good idea," she says. Jen, Lori, and I are silent, waiting. I think they're just as shocked as I am over what's happening.

"Her grandmother let me in, but I can't say Hayley looked too pleased to see me. She was rude right from the start and only got worse as I tried to talk to her. I told her we were all worried about her."

"We really *are*," I agree. Jen meets my eye and nods.

"Yeah, well, she wasn't one bit interested in hearing that." Carrie pauses and pokes at the poutine she bought for lunch. She takes a small bite and chews it quickly before going on.

"So, apparently, this has been coming for a while. The sad truth is that Hayley doesn't like *any* of us anymore. Actually, judging by the things she said, she really hates us. You should have heard the way she sounded."

"What kind of things did she say?" Lori prods.

Carrie shakes her head while she eats another bite of poutine. "Horrible things. Horrible and mean," she tells us. "I hate to repeat any of it, but I guess you have the right to know."

She turns toward Jen first. "I *really* don't like to say this, because I think you look great just the way you are. But Hayley said she can't stand eating lunch with you. She said it makes her sick, the way you stuff food into your fat face at lunch."

I'm shocked, and I can see by the others' faces that they are, too. Jen is always worrying about her weight, but the idea that she's fat is totally in her head. She has some crazy idea that she should be skin and bones like a model.

She turns her head away now, but not before the rest of us see tears filling her eyes. Anger flares up inside me at Hayley. And it gets worse.

Carrie goes on to tell us the other terrible things that Hayley said to her. Like, how Lori is the most selfish, stuck-up person she's ever met, and Krysti is a skank who wears the shortest skirts she can find because she wants all the guys to know she's open for business.

Then she gets to me. I try to steel myself, but nothing can prepare me for what I hear next.

"And Shana," Carrie says. Her voice drops and she can't look at me as she repeats Hayley's hateful words. "She said Shana is the worst of all of us because she goes around acting like miss-goody-two-shoes, but then she went and made out with a greaseball like Sly Blackwood."

"What?" Lori says with a gasp. "Ewww. That's not true, is it, Shana?"

I want to deny it, but my mouth won't move. And even if I could speak, I'd be lying if I said it never happened.

It wasn't long after Mike and I broke up. As in, right after he dumped me. Everything hurt so much. So, I did something stupid. I had a pity party and got wasted one Saturday when my mom and dad were out for the evening. All I originally intended to do was dull the pain and go to sleep. I can't remember when or how that changed but all of a sudden I decided it was a much better plan to go to Mike's house. I had this crazy idea that if I confronted him and he saw how much I was hurting, he'd change his mind and want to get back together.

So, I was on my way there, lurching along the street. Only, partway there I lost momentum. All I wanted to do was put my head down and rest. I guess that's when I ran into Sly, and the next thing I knew, I was at his place. Then I was laying on his bed while the room spun around me. I'm not sure how it happened that we started kissing, but we did. That went on for a while

— until I felt his hand snaking its way under my top. By the time he'd reached my bra the fog had cleared enough for me to protest. Rather loudly, in fact. My drunken yelling brought his older sister to the scene and she lit into him, too. Then she got me into a car and drove me home.

My cheeks feel like there are flames burning against them as I remember that night. I can hardly face the others, who have already realized that my red-faced silence means what Carrie just said is true. I, Shana Tremain, have made out with the scruffiest guy in our entire school. Close as we are, that isn't something I ever wanted to share with my friends.

And that's when it hits me. I *never* told *Hayley* about Sly. There's only one person in the whole world who I shared that ugly moment in my life with.

My very best friend. Carrie Freeman.

CHAPTER NINE

I'm so nervous that I can hardly steady my finger to ring the doorbell. The second I hear the corresponding buzz inside, I wish I could take it back, turn, and run.

What am I doing here?

The door swings open with a long squeak. Hayley's grandfather is standing there. He smiles warmly and tells me he'll fetch Hayley. He goes back inside and disappears around the corner. I hear him telling Hayley that someone is there to see her.

She doesn't look happy to see me, but she doesn't yell or tell me to get out or anything. I offer a weak smile.

"Hi, Hayley," I say. She just stares. I take a deep breath and go on. "Remember that day in the cafeteria — when you told me you didn't know who you could trust?"

She nods, still looking wary.

"*Me*," I say. It sounds louder than I meant it to. "You can trust me."

Hayley's expression softens just a little. She steps back and gestures for me to come in. As

I step inside, her grandmother's head appears down the hall a little, where the doorway opens to the kitchen.

"Oh, hello, Shana," she calls. "Hayley, should I make you girls something to snack on?"

"We're good, Gram, thanks, anyway," Hayley tells her. "We're just going to hang out in my room for a while."

"Well, you just email me a text message if you change your mind," her grandmother says, waving her cellphone in the air.

"Okay, Gram," Hayley tells her, while we try not to giggle. Then she whispers to me, "Gram's awfully proud of how tech-savvy she is. I don't have the heart to correct her."

"It must be hard for old people to keep all this stuff straight," I say. I can't help wondering how a girl who won't hurt her grandmother's feelings by telling her you don't email a text message could be so cruel to her friends.

We get to Hayley's room and she points me to her desk chair and then plunks down on the end of her bed. "So," she says, "you wanted to talk to me?"

I've been thinking about how to approach this. I don't want to betray Carrie, but I'm bothered by what she claims Hayley said about me. Mainly, I can't figure out how Hayley knew about Sly.

I suppose it's possible that Sly blabbed and Hayley heard it from somewhere else. I'm doubtful about that, though. I'd called him and begged him to keep it between us after I realized what I'd done. I know he was totally embarrassed at the way it ended, so luckily he would have had his own reasons for keeping it quiet, too. In any case, he'd been super-nice about it and promised he wouldn't tell. I never heard a whisper about it from anyone, so I'm pretty sure he kept his word. After all, if he'd blabbed it around, it's almost guaranteed that it would have gotten back to me.

Another possibility is that Carrie betrayed my confidence and told Hayley about it at some point in time. But that doesn't make sense to me, either. Carrie is closer to Jen and Krysti than she is to Hayley, but they clearly hadn't heard it before now. If Carrie was going to tell one other person in our group, I can't see it being Hayley.

If neither of those things happened, there's only one other possibility. It's the last thing I want to be true, but I'm determined to find out, one way or the other. What I need to do is find out the truth from Hayley, if I can. I turn to face her.

"So," I say, drawing it out, "about Sly Blackwood."

"Sly Blackwood?" she repeats, like I've just said something in a strange language. "What about him?"

"You said something about him to Carrie," I say, vaguely.

"About Sly Blackwood?" she echoes. She looks as puzzled as she sounds. "What are you talking about, Shana? I thought you were here to discuss what's going on."

It's as clear to me as it's ever going to be. Hayley obviously has no idea what I'm talking about. There's no way she said what Carrie claims she said. That brings me to my next question.

"Did Carrie come here to see you the other day?"

"Yes." Hayley's expression stiffens. I can almost see her thinking she'd better be careful what she says to me.

"What did she want?" I ask.

Hayley's eyes lift to meet mine. "What did she want?" she says. "She wanted to let me know how the rest of you felt. That you didn't want anything more to do with me, since you all apparently believe I've been stealing from you."

"And that's what she told you?" I ask. I'm not nearly as shocked as I should be, so I guess I suspected something like this.

"Well, I've left out the nasty details, but yes, that's what she told me."

"It's a lie," I say.

"A lie?"

"Absolutely. In fact, it's the opposite of what she was supposed to tell you."

Hayley has slumped a little. I lean forward, reaching across the space between us, and put my hand on her arm. I start talking and I don't stop until I've told her everything. She's the most shocked by the things Carrie claims she said about the rest of us.

"I would *never* say any of those things!" she cries. "You're my friends."

"I know. And I believe you," I say. "And I know you didn't steal anything, either."

Hayley jumps up and crosses the short space to where I'm sitting. She hugs me and begins to cry.

"I felt so alone," she says between sobs. "I thought she'd managed to turn everyone against me. And I didn't know what to do about it. It looked so bad — especially when your brooch turned up in my bag. And Carrie was so convincing."

I think about how Carrie pretended to believe Hayley might have hidden the piece of jewellery in the house. At the time, that had helped dispel any doubts I had. It made the case against Hayley so much more convincing, which, of course, is why she did it.

But, I realize suddenly, it had done more than just convince the rest of us. It had also thrown Hayley off guard.

"When Carrie said I might have hidden it, I thought that's what she'd done," Hayley says, confirming what I'm thinking. "She tricked me into feeling safe about dumping out my bag."

She sits back on the edge of the bed. She's composed again, but still looking sad. "I don't know if the others will believe the truth," she says. "Either way, our group is ruined."

She's right. I feel sick, wondering what will happen next. Mostly, though, I'm puzzled.

"There's one thing I can't seem to figure out," I admit.

"What's that?"

"*Why?* Why did Carrie do any of this?"

"Oh, I think I know *exactly* why she did it," Hayley says.

CHAPTER TEN

"Carrie has been uneasy around me for a while," Hayley says. She's speaking slowly and her voice is subdued. "I've felt her watching me, wondering what to do about the threat I pose to her."

"*Threat?*" I repeat. "What do you mean?"

"I think Carrie was worried about something she said to me a year ago." Hayley pauses. I can see that she's struggling with what to say next. I wait silently.

"Remember the boarder my grandparents had for a while?" she says.

"The guy with the really bushy eyebrows?" I ask.

"That's the one. Anyway, he gave me the creeps. Something about him just *bothered* me."

I nod, thinking back. Hayley had told us this guy's presence made her really uncomfortable when he'd rented a room at her grandparents' house. I'd only met him a couple of times, but I could totally see what she meant. He had a way of coming into a room that reminded me of a snake slithering around. His eyes were small and dark and when he pointed them at you,

you could almost feel how cold they were. The worst thing, though, was his mouth. He had the thinnest lips I've ever seen, and they looked as if they were always just about to sneer.

"He didn't stay all that long, did he?" I ask.

"Four months," she answers. "It seemed a lot longer than that, believe me. I spent as much time in my room as I could, just to avoid him. I was *so* glad when he got his own apartment and moved out."

She pauses to offer a slightly embarrassed smile. "Looking back, I feel silly about it. I mean, he was never mean or rude or anything to me. There was no reason for me to feel the way I did."

"He looked pretty creepy," I remind her.

"I guess that was the whole thing. And the poor guy couldn't help the way he looked."

"My mom always says you should never judge a person by appearance. Even a serial killer can look like someone you would totally trust."

"True," Hayley says.

There is silence then, for a moment or two. A shadow seems to pass over Hayley's face. I can see that she wants to speak, but she hesitates.

"So … you were going to tell me something about the things that have been happening?" I ask.

"You mean the things Carrie has been doing," Hayley says evenly.

"Right," I say. Everything we've already talked about has left me feeling like a traitor. I wonder if Hayley can sense that.

"I know she's your best friend, Shana. How do I know I can *really* trust you?"

"Because I'm here," I tell her. "Because I could have just ignored the things that were bothering me. But I didn't."

"There's more to this than just Carrie, though," she answers. "And I'm not quite sure whose side you're going to be on when you hear the whole thing."

"Well, I can't *make* you trust me," I say. I'm getting impatient and just a little angry that she's hedging. I've already taken her side against my best friend. You'd think that would be enough for her to be sure of me.

Hayley draws in a deep breath. Her cheeks bulge as she lets it out slowly. Then she shrugs and says, "I guess I have no choice. And really, what else do I have to lose?"

She picks up a throw pillow and hugs it to her stomach, like she needs something for comfort, or support. And then she tells me the whole story.

"It was last year, when the boarder we were just talking about was here. I guess he'd been living at the house for a couple of months by then. So, this one afternoon, Carrie came by to pick up some DVDs she was borrowing from me, and he was kicking around the house. He wasn't bothering us or anything, but I noticed her glancing at him. Later on, when he wasn't around anymore, she mentioned him. I told her how creepy I found him."

Hayley gets up and goes to her window. She stands there, looking out, her back to me. I want to tell her to hurry up and finish the story. I can't see how it could have anything to do with what Carrie has been doing. That makes me curious about what the connection could possibly be.

"I told Carrie that I wished my grandparents would get rid of him," Hayley continues after a moment. "But I'd already told them I didn't like him, and they just said I was being silly. That's when Carrie said if I really hated having him there, she knew how I could get rid of him."

Hayley turns from the window and looks me straight in the eye. "She told me it would be easy. All I had to do was say he molested me and that would be the end of him."

My heart begins to pound hard in my chest. I feel like I can't quite breathe. Suddenly, I can't look at her. I know she's aware of my reaction, but she doesn't comment on it.

"So my theory," she continues, "is that she's worried I think that's what she did with her stepfather. It was no secret that she didn't want him around."

"Carrie wouldn't do that," I insist. My voice sounds strange.

"Well, even if she *would* do it," Hayley says, "I guess that's not what happened. After all, she had a *witness*, didn't she? *You* saw him touch her."

CHAPTER ELEVEN

I can't answer. There are so many thoughts rushing through my head that it's impossible to sort them out. I need time to think.

"That's what you testified to, isn't it?" Hayley asks after a bit. "That you saw Joe Kelward touch Carrie?"

"Yes," I say.

"So it's like this," Hayley says. "I don't trust Carrie. At all. I've seen her set people up too many times over the years. And you know what I'm talking about. The little whispering campaigns. The lies and twisted stories. She manipulates people into doing her dirty work all the time."

I hate to admit how much truth there is in what she's saying. But when you're friends with someone, you let stuff like that slide. Sometimes you even buy into it a little.

"But when I heard that you were going to testify, that was different," Hayley tells me. "Unless, of course, she talked you into it somehow."

Her words hang there between us. I know she's waiting, giving me a chance to deny it. It would be so easy. All I have to do is open my mouth and tell her that didn't happen. But I can't. There have been enough lies.

On the other hand, it's not that easy to admit the truth, either. I know I'm not going to get away with saying nothing. After everything that's just happened, Hayley deserves an answer. More than that, she deserves the truth.

"She asked me to help her," I say. It sounds lame.

"To help her by lying in court ... under oath," Hayley says.

"Yes." It's a bit of a relief to admit it. To get it out. I hadn't realized, until this moment, how much it was bothering me.

"That man went to prison," Hayley says, like I need someone to tell me.

"I know that," I answer. "But maybe he really did do something to her."

"Right."

"It's possible," I insist. "You didn't see her when she told me about it. She was a mess — crying and shaking and scared."

"I just bet," Hayley says.

"But really, Hayley. You didn't see her that day. She was seriously upset."

"Oh, I've seen Carrie upset lots of times," Hayley says with a sharp laugh. "Like the time she got caught dumping garbage on her neighbours' lawn. Remember how she went on, telling them how sorry she was and begging them not to call the cops. And then when they let her off she laughed behind their backs and called them suckers."

I remember it all right. Hayley and Jen and I had been at Carrie's place when the couple who live two houses away from her came knocking on the door. They accused her of throwing trash in their yard. Carrie denied knowing anything about it until they produced some mail that had been in among the garbage. It was addressed to her parents, so they had her solid. I forget exactly why she did it. She takes things the wrong way sometimes, so it probably wasn't over much.

Hayley's right. Carrie had put on quite a show of how sorry she was when the neighbours showed up. And it really had been nothing but an act. But I can't believe she was acting when she told me about her stepfather.

"I know what you're saying," I tell Hayley. "But you weren't there. You didn't see the tears or hear the way she was sobbing."

Hayley throws her hands up and shrugs. "You just believe whatever you need to," she says. "But remember that if you're wrong, the man you helped put in prison might be innocent."

I feel like I've been punched hard in the stomach. There is silence in the room for a few moments. I try to convince myself that there's no way Carrie would do anything that horrible. This isn't some prank, some slightly destructive bit of revenge. It's a man's life — his honour and his freedom. It's unthinkable that my best friend could do something that evil.

"I don't know what to do," I finally confess.

Hayley crosses to me and slings an arm around my shoulder. "You have to find out the truth," she says.

"How? There are only two people in the world who really know what the truth is. One of them is locked up. So, what do I do, just go and ask Carrie? Like she would ever admit it if she's been lying the whole time."

"Yeah, I don't think it would be very smart to say anything to Carrie," Hayley says. "If she even *suspects* that you doubt her, watch out."

I want to say that Carrie is my best friend, that she would never do anything to hurt me. But I can't.

"So, what do I do?" I ask. "There's no way I can find out the truth."

"Maybe not about that," Hayley admits. "But there are other things."

"Like what?"

"Like the stolen jewellery. I know *I* didn't take it, but stuff *did* go missing."

"So, you think Carrie has it?" I ask.

"Yes, I do. Either that or she got rid of it. I already wondered if she might have planted stuff here, but I looked everywhere I could think of and there was nothing."

"I don't think she'd get rid of anything," I say. "She'd be more likely to show up with it one day and claim she forced you to give it back."

Hayley doesn't look convinced. "You know what? I bet she plans to keep it. Think about what she took. We know about Lori's ring — the one her dad gave her. And even though she was setting me up, she took that brooch your great-grandmother left you. It looks like there might be a pattern there — that she's taking things that have sentimental value."

"So that makes you think she's more likely to keep the stuff?" I ask.

"Absolutely. I bet it makes her feel powerful to own things that other people value that way — things they can't replace."

"That's horrible," I say.

"*Carrie* is horrible," Hayley snaps. "A lot of things about her have bothered me for a while now, especially in the past year or so. Mean things she did, and sneaky. But I never wanted to say anything. I figured, let it go — why cause trouble in our group?"

I guess there have been a few times I've been bothered by something Carrie has done, too, but

I'm still not quite ready to believe the worst of her. There have, after all, been a lot of good things, as well. It's hard for me to think so badly of someone who's been my best friend for so long.

CHAPTER TWELVE

In the end, Hayley and I come up with a general kind of plan. First of all, we agree that alerting Carrie to my suspicions would be the dumbest thing I could do. Besides, if it turns out this is all just a crazy theory that turns out to be wrong, then I won't have ruined my friendship with her for nothing.

I will act like everything is perfectly normal. I'll hang out with Carrie and the others as usual and I won't have anything to do with Hayley when there's anyone else around. I need to get into Carrie's house and look for chances to find the missing jewellery. If I find it, I'll tell the others and confront her with the evidence.

That still doesn't answer the questions running through my head about Joe Kelward. I know I'm going to need to face that soon, but it's not exactly something I'm looking forward to.

I feel awkward the next day at school, but no one seems to notice anything is wrong. I relax after a couple of minutes and manage to pay attention to the conversation.

Jen is talking about a tattoo. Nothing new there. About once a month she announces that she's found The One, the tattoo she's going to get as soon as she turns eighteen. Her folks won't give her permission to get one before then. That's probably a good thing, considering how often she changes her mind.

Today's choice is a tiny pink dragon. Jen is undecided if she's going to get it on her ankle or her shoulder. None of us comment on that. We all know she has three years to change her mind. We also know the dragon will probably be forgotten before she turns sixteen, never mind eighteen.

The talk shifts to last night's TV shows, then moves through a string of topics that slip by before I've fully focused on them. It's all so normal. I begin to relax.

Carrie is seated across from me, paying less attention to the talk than to the chicken Caesar salad she's having for lunch. When she happens to glance up and sees me watching her, she just smiles — an everyday smile you'd give a friend — and goes back to her lunch.

And the day passes.

I see Hayley a couple of times as we pass each other in the halls on the way to our different classes. We ignore each other completely, as we've agreed to do. It's essential that Carrie believes she's been successful in cutting off all contact between Hayley and the rest of us.

It's a relief to hear the final bell ring. I'd never realized just how hard it is to put on an act all day, or to walk around carrying a secret this heavy. It would be nice to go home and relax for the evening, but the sooner I can look for the missing jewellery at Carrie's place, the better. So, I catch her on the way out of the school and suggest we hang out this evening.

"Yeah, sure," she says. "Perfect, in fact. Mom just texted me that she's working late again."

"You want to come to my place to eat first?" I ask.

"Maybe. What's your mom making?"

I make a quick call home, ask Mom, and then report that it's tuna casserole.

Carrie wrinkles her nose and says "No, thanks."

"Then, I'll see you later," I tell her. I'm relieved that she's not coming. My parents like all of my friends, but since the whole business with Carrie's stepfather they've been extra nice to her. The thought of them being all sympathetic and caring toward her after what I've just learned makes me sick.

It's just after seven when I get to her place. The side door is unlocked and when I knock I hear a yell. I take it as permission to go in. Noise from the front room draws me there, where I find Carrie sprawled across the couch watching television. Some reality show.

"Hey, Shana," she says with a half wave. She's clearly less interested in my arrival than in what she's watching.

I sink into an armchair and wonder how much longer the show is. A strange lump grows in my throat as I sit there, in a chair I've occupied so many times. An urge comes over me to ask Carrie about everything that's been happening. I want her to offer an explanation even though I know very well that there is none. I want everything to be okay, and for Carrie to still be the friend I've believed she was for the past three years. But in my heart, I know that's not going to happen.

A commercial comes on and Carrie stretches, turns to face me, and grins. "Sorry," she says. "You know how addicted I am to reality TV."

I force a smile. "Sure, no problem," I tell her. Then inspiration hits me. This is the perfect time to start looking around — while Carrie's engrossed in the show she's watching. I wait until the commercials end and then casually ask if I can borrow a sweater.

"Sure," she says without looking away from the TV. "Get whatever you want."

I go to her room, feeling guilty. It gets worse as I open her dresser drawers and run my hands along the bottom of each one, trying not to mess up the contents in the process. At the same time, I'm trying to listen for any sound of metal clinking, in case there's anything hidden in among her clothes. And, of course, I'm listening for any sound in the hallway, just in case Carrie tears herself away from the show and comes along.

I find nothing in the dresser or her desk. The closet is next and by now I'm so nervous that my skin feels a bit prickly. Even before I open the door I know it's going to be hopeless. You never saw a closet stuffed so full! Besides being jammed with clothes hanging from the rod, there are more bags and boxes than you'd think a person could squeeze into a space this size. I poke at a few things half-heartedly but I know there's no way I can go through even a tenth of what's in there. Instead, I stand there staring, like there might be clues that will jump out and tell me where to start. If there's anything that might give away a secret hiding place, it sure isn't obvious to me. And I've been in her room long enough that Carrie is bound to start wondering what's up. There's no choice but to give up for now.

I sigh and start to close the door, but then I remember that I'm supposed to be getting a sweater, so I yank it back open. And that's when I hear it.

On the inside of her closet door, Carrie has a hanging shoe holder. It's red vinyl, kind of ugly, with sixteen compartments. There are a few pair of slippers stuffed into the compartments, but most of them hold other things. There are scarves, hand fans, ornaments that have fallen out of favour and an assortment of other odds and ends.

And something that made a metallic tinkling sound when I jerked the door.

I run my hands along the bottoms of each row of shoe pockets, feeling the contents as quickly as I can. I find what I'm looking for in a pocket holding Carrie's old Brownie sash and badges. Tucked in the bottom is a small collection of jewellery. It takes only a quick glance through it before I recognize Lori's ring.

I have my proof.

CHAPTER THIRTEEN

If I were in a movie right now, this would be the moment where Carrie would appear in the doorway. She'd demand to know what I thought I was doing and I'd stand there like a mannequin with its mouth stuck open, trying to think of something to say.

Fortunately, this isn't a movie and no one comes along. I hesitate for a second and then shove the jewellery back where it was, grab a sweater, and hurry back to the front room. Another batch of commercials is on and Carrie is sitting up, looking around.

"I can't find the remote," she says. "I had it just a minute ago and now it's gone."

"You're probably sitting on it," I suggest.

She stands up and turns to inspect the couch. The remote is half hidden between cushions and she digs it out.

"Good thinking," she says, waving it. She flops back down and then thinks to ask, "What took you so long to get a sweater?"

"Sorry. I was texting."

"Oh, yeah? Who was it? Was it Krysti? I've

been trying to get ahold of her since I got home."

"No, not Krysti," I say. I feel my face getting warm. "It was, uh, my cousin. You don't know her."

"You're the absolute worst liar of anyone I know," she says, laughing. "It's like you're wearing a big sign that says you're lying. So, really, who was it? Was it Jake? It *was*, wasn't it? I told you he was going to make a move."

I'm trying to think of what to say when the commercial break ends and her attention shifts back to the television.

I wish I could leave. The idea of spending the evening with her after what I've just discovered makes me feel a little ill. I even toy with the idea of telling her I'm sick, but I don't want to do anything that might make her suspicious. So I stay, and when her show ends we hang out until my school-night curfew.

When I hit the sidewalk to head home, my knees are almost rubbery with relief to be out of there. I gulp fresh air like I've been breathing something toxic, which is exactly how I feel.

The question is: what do I do next? The temptation to confront Carrie with the stolen jewellery had been almost overpowering, but I know it would have been a bad mistake. She'd have denied knowing anything about it.

She'd likely have tried to claim that Hayley was setting her up.

And, honestly, I'm afraid she'd have worn me down. Carrie can be so persuasive and once she starts she goes on and on until she's won. I've been there before, although never over anything this serious.

If I'm going to confront her, I need the others present. It's almost certain that she won't be able to persuade everyone.

When I get home I give Hayley a quick call. When she hears that I've found the stolen items, her voice begins to quaver.

"I thought it was hopeless, and I'd lost my friends for good," she says. "You have no idea how grateful I am that you believed me, Shana."

We talk a few more minutes before she brings up the big question.

"So, does this mean you're going to go to the police and tell them the truth about Joe Kelward?"

"I guess I have no choice," I say. "I just wish there was some way I could find out one hundred percent that Carrie made that up. I mean, isn't it possible that she's telling the truth?"

"Then why set me up the way she did?"

"Maybe she was just worried you'd *think* she made it up — because of what she said to you about the boarder."

"I hope you know how lame that sounds," Hayley says. "Who would come up with such a complicated plan if they weren't guilty?"

"You're right. I guess I'm just scared."

"I don't imagine Carrie's stepfather is feeling all that great, either," she says dryly.

Shame fills me at the thought of Joe Kelward. If he's truly innocent — and I'm pretty well convinced he is — it must be horrible for him. Imagine being locked up in prison for something you didn't do. Especially when that something is a crime as disgusting as molesting your own stepdaughter. How horrible and helpless and angry he must feel.

"Anyway, Shana," Hayley continues, "you don't need to be sure about whether or not Carrie made it all up before you do something."

"What do you mean?" I ask.

"I mean that there's at least one thing you *do* know. You know that *your* testimony was a lie. And *that's* what you need to tell the police."

There's dead air on the phone for the next minute. I know Hayley's waiting for me to speak. I find my voice at last, and it's a cowardly one.

"What do you think will happen when I tell them?" I ask.

"I have no idea. I just know you have to do the right thing. It's terrible, what's happened to that man — and honestly, I never thought he did what she said. You've got to do whatever you can to make it right."

"I know I do," I say.

"You should start by talking to your parents," Hayley adds. "They're going to have to know, and they can probably give you some advice."

That suggestion fills me with hope and dread all at the same time. I don't know how I can face my mom and dad and admit what I've done. On the other hand, if anyone will know what's likely to happen, it's my true-crime-expert mother.

I'm off the phone and almost ready to take a deep breath and go confess everything to my parents when I realize something else that makes me call Hayley back.

"What about the jewellery?" I ask as soon as she answers. "If I go to the police now, they'll talk to Carrie. She'll know I'm not on her side anymore. That will mean I won't have a chance to expose her as the real thief."

"Oh! Right," she says. "You need to take care of that first, don't you?"

"Definitely."

"Well, then, you have to do something about that as soon as you can," she says.

"I will. Promise. It shouldn't be a problem, anyway. We're all supposed to get together at Carrie's place on the weekend. I'll figure out what to do by then."

"Look, Shana, I know I'm being pushy about this."

"It's okay," I tell her. "I understand why."

"I don't want you to be mad at me," she adds. "You're the only friend I have left."

"I swear, I'm not mad, Hayley. I get it."

After I hang up I feel so totally exhausted that all I can do is crawl into bed and fall asleep. The last thought on my mind is that I wish I could go back in time and undo my part in this whole mess.

CHAPTER FOURTEEN

Saturday is *finally* here. Honestly, I don't know how I've gotten through the week. Now I've just arrived at Carrie's place, and I'm about as nervous as a person could possibly be. No wonder, since I've spent the whole day thinking about what I'm about to do. It's one of those things you can't plan too much, because you never know how it's all going to play out. I've tried to imagine how the others will react when I "find" the jewellery in Carrie's closet, but the only thing I can really picture is Carrie trying to deny everything.

Everyone else is already there except Lori, and she shows up fifteen minutes later, breathless from hurrying.

"My mom picked today to make me clean out the aquarium," she explains. "I swear she does things like that on purpose when she knows I have somewhere to go."

"Sure she does. She knows that's the only way she can actually get you to *do* anything," Jen says. She laughs when Lori pretends to be insulted.

It tugs at my heart, seeing the easy friendship, the way they know and understand each other — just the way it was with me and Carrie such a short time ago. As angry as I am over everything she's done, I have to admit there's a horrible ache in me, knowing I'm about to do something that will end our friendship forever. It seems strange, to care after all I've learned in the past few days, but I do.

I'm here today for one reason only. I need a chance to confront Carrie about the jewellery. The only thing that has to happen first is for all of us to be in her room, and this happens almost right away, when Lori suggests we do designs on each others' toenails. Carrie has a huge supply of polish and stickers, so we all gather in her room to pick out colours and nail art.

It's a perfect opportunity because her nail supplies are in a plastic bin that she keeps in her closet. She opens the door and kneels down to pull it out, which is when I step forward.

"Hey, what's this?" I ask as I reach toward the shoe holder and dip into the pocket with the Brownie sash and badges. I tug them out, trying to look casual.

"I didn't know you were ever a Brownie," I say, hoping my voice sounds normal. "Are these all your badges, or are there more?" I dip my hand back into the pocket like I'm checking.

My fingers reach and touch the bottom and find ... nothing!

Confusion floods me. I look toward Carrie automatically and find her watching me with hard, cold eyes. There's a smirk twitching at the corner of her mouth.

"Were you looking for *this* by any chance?"

I turn to find the others staring at me. Krysti is between Lori and Jen, and she's holding out her hand. Clustered in her outstretched palm is the missing jewellery.

"I wondered what you were *really* doing in my room the other day when you were here," Carrie says. She's fought the smirk off and now looks like she's on the verge of tears. "Then I noticed a badge on the floor and when I went to put it back, I found the stuff you'd planted."

"I didn't plant anything," I say, "It was already there!"

"Sure it was," Krysti snaps. "Carrie called me right after you left that day. She told me what she'd found. It was obvious to both of us exactly what you were planning to do and you just proved we were right. What I don't understand is why you'd do this to Carrie."

"I'm trying to understand it, too," Carrie says. "I have a feeling that Hayley put you up to this, Shana. I just don't know how she convinced you. Does she have something on you?

How could you try to set me up like that, when we've been best friends for so long?"

"The only person who was set up tonight was *me* and you know it," I say. I feel as though I'm watching a scene that's happening to someone else. Lori and Jen are clearly shocked, but I can see that they believe what Carrie and Krysti are saying.

All eyes are on me as I stand there, mouth flapping and nothing else coming out. As I look around at them I see that Carrie's eyes are laughing at me. Her face is smug and triumphant, although I know that expression will disappear and she'll go back to her big act the second anyone else turns toward her again.

"You know what you are? You're pure *evil*," I say, keeping my gaze level on her. I have nothing to offer the others to prove my innocence and I know it would be pointless to try. This room is full of hostility and betrayal and the only thing left for me to do is leave.

I pick up my bag and make my way to the door. Behind me, I hear the buzz of whispers. My throat is tight and tears are threatening to come, but I take deep breaths and fight to stay composed.

As I make my way toward the sidewalk, something makes me turn and look up at the house. And there she is, watching from a window. It's easy to imagine how she managed that. I can picture her telling the others she needed a few moments alone. They would have been so sympathetic toward her as she slipped out of the room, pretending to be overcome with sadness over my deceitfulness.

A smile breaks across her face when she sees me looking at her. She lifts a hand and wiggles her fingers in a strangely gleeful wave. I don't move. I stand there, stone-faced, staring at her as she conducts her bizarre performance. I wonder if I ever knew the real Carrie Freeman at all.

It's amazing, what that moment does for me. It's like I've been living in an illusion all this time, seeing her as one person when in reality she was someone else altogether. Any feelings of regret I have slide away.

I don't blame the others — not even Krysti. They're just more victims of Carrie's lies and manipulation. If any of them found her out and dared to cross her, she would turn on them just as surely as she turned on Hayley and me.

There's one thing puzzling me, though. I can't figure out what alerted Carrie to the fact that I'd found the stolen jewellery in that holder. Today, she claimed that she'd found one of the badges was on the floor, but I know that wasn't true. I was super careful to make sure there was nothing left around that would give me away.

Unfortunately, the only person who knows the answer to that is Carrie. Somehow, I don't think I'm likely to get the truth out of her.

CHAPTER FIFTEEN

I'm not looking forward to telling Hayley what happened, but I can't think of a reason to put it off. I call her when I get home.

Her voice sounds just as disappointed as I expect. We had both hoped that exposing Carrie as the real thief would make everything right with the rest of the group.

"Now what?" she asks.

"Now I go to the police and tell them the truth about my testimony," I say. "There's nothing else we can do about what's happened between us and our other friends. And actually, I feel guilty that I put *that* off for something so much less important, especially with the way things turned out."

"At least you tried," she says. "And one good thing came of it, anyway."

"What's that?"

"Lori got her ring back."

"That's true," I say. "That actually makes me feel a little bit better."

"Me, too. That ring means so much to her. I remember how upset she was when it went missing."

I remember, too — and that makes me even angrier at Carrie. How could she have done something that mean to a friend? It makes me wonder, if I hadn't found the stolen things in her room — would Lori ever have gotten her ring back? Somehow, I doubt it.

I end the call with Hayley and wander down the hall to the laundry room. Mom is in there ironing. I tell her that I need to talk to her and Dad when she's done. She turns off the iron that very second and goes to get him. She tells me to go to the living room and that they'll be right there.

It's so awkward — I wish I'd suggested the kitchen instead. I'm sitting in the armchair while they're across from me, sitting close to one another on the couch. Their faces are worried.

"I didn't mean to scare you," I start, "but I have something to tell you and it's kind of serious. It's about Joe Kelward."

"He *did* do something to you!" my mom says. She grabs my dad's hand and looks like she's going to burst into tears.

"No!" I say quickly, before my dad can start saying things like he'd like to get his hands on the creep for five minutes. "No, it's nothing like that. Could you please, just let me explain everything before you say anything else?"

They promise to listen, and they actually do pretty well. I go over the whole thing, about how Carrie told me he was molesting her, and how she begged me to back her story up. I admit that my testimony was a lie. I explain that I totally believed her, but that now I'm almost positive that she was lying. I tell them what I learned from Hayley, and how Carrie turned our friends against Hayley with the jewellery thefts, to keep Hayley from telling anyone about her suspicions.

It's a relief to get it all out, but I wish my mom and dad didn't look quite so horrified. It's Dad who speaks first.

"That man went to prison, Shana. To *prison*."

"I know, Dad. I'm so sorry — and I want to do whatever it takes to make it right."

"It may not be that easy," Mom says. Her mouth quivers and I can see she's still on the verge of crying. "It's not always a simple matter of telling the truth and everything is okay."

"What do you mean?" I ask.

"I, well, I guess this kind of thing is handled differently in different places," she says after a pause. "The best thing to do is go ahead and talk to the police and see what happens from there."

"What kind of trouble do you think Shana will be in?" Dad asks her.

"It's hard to say. She's a minor, and she didn't do it out of malice. But she did commit perjury, which is serious. I don't know whether she'll be charged or not, but they certainly have grounds if they want to. The only thing in her favour is that she's a minor. They may take that into consideration."

"It doesn't matter, anyway," I say, trying to sound braver than I feel. "Whatever happens to me is my own fault. The only thing that's really important is that Mr. Kelward is freed."

Dad nods at that. Then he turns back to Mom and asks, "Do you think Shana should have an attorney present when she talks to the police?"

"I don't know. It would probably be enough if one of us goes with her when she talks to them."

It hadn't occurred to me that my mom or dad might come with me when I go to the police to confess what I've done. I can't quite tell if I'm relieved or dismayed. Not that it makes any difference. And at this point, all I want is for it to be over with.

CHAPTER SIXTEEN

My stomach lurches as our car turns onto Gottingen Street and pulls up to the Regional Police station. I take a few slow, deep breaths to calm myself, but it doesn't help much.

It turns out that it's Dad who's with me. For all of Mom's true-crime knowledge, she decided she was too emotional to go and would probably cause more problems than anything. Dad gives me a quick smile of encouragement as we climb the steps and approach the red brick building where the vice team has its offices. Once inside, we give our names and are told to wait and that someone will be with us shortly.

"Shortly" turns out to be about forty minutes. I've gone to the bathroom to pee twice in that time and am just thinking a third trip might be necessary when an officer appears and takes us to an interview room. I'm relieved that it's not the same one who took my statement against Mr. Kelward. I remember, with shame, how kind that officer was. After I'd given him my statement he patted my hand and told me I had done the right thing.

Today, it's Officer Plourde, an older man who looks like he's forgotten how to smile. Frown creases are etched on his face and his manner is gruff as he tells us to take a seat. Once he's seated himself at the other side of the table, he flips open a notepad and asks how he can help us.

It's hard to begin and my voice wavers a few times. Dad gives me nod and pats my shoulder to let me know it's okay, but the steely eyes of Officer Plourde offer no encouragement. Slowly, painfully, I get the facts out — how I had given false information to the police and on the witness stand, believing I was helping my friend. I told him I'd come to believe Carrie's story was a lie, and that I was convinced her stepfather had done nothing wrong and should not be in prison.

Officer Plourde jots down a few things as I talk. He lets me finish before he has any questions for me. Then, the things he asks surprise me.

"You say that you made up your testimony to help your friend, Carrie Freeman?" he says.

"Yes."

"How long have you two been friends?"

"About three years."

"And has there been any change in your relationship with Carrie recently?"

"We're not friends now," I say. I wonder if I should have told him about the jewellery and everything that happened over it, but Dad had told me not to go into that. He'd said I shouldn't make it too complicated.

"I see," Officer Plourde says. He doesn't sound like he sees at all. His eyes narrow and he leans forward just a little.

"Are you aware that it's a serious thing to make a false statement to the police?" he asks.

"Yes." My voice is barely a whisper.

"Well, in that case, do you want to reconsider anything about what you just told me?"

I stare at him, not understanding. Is he trying to give me a way out? Does he mean to suggest that I should forget about it, and leave an innocent man to a fate he doesn't deserve?

"I'm not quite sure what you're getting at," my dad says. He looks just as confused as I feel. "My daughter came in here to do the right thing. She knows there will be consequences and she's ready to accept them."

Officer Plourde sighs and throws his hands up. "Okay," he says. "But we have a problem. A big one." He lets that sink in for a few seconds before he continues. "Fact is, we're already aware of the situation between you and your friend, uh, Ms. Freeman. She was in to see us a few days ago. Young lady was quite upset and worried. She told us there had been some trouble over the theft of some rings and things. When she realized you were involved she tried to talk to you about it, which is when you threatened to come here and make trouble for her. According to Ms. Freeman, you said you were going to do everything you could to see that her molester was freed to hurt her again."

"That's a lie!" I tell him. "*Carrie* is the one who stole the jewellery. She was setting up Hayley, because Hayley knew Carrie made up the story about her stepfather."

"And how did Hayley know that?" Officer Plourde asks. He sounds skeptical.

I try to explain about the boarder and Carrie's suggestion to Hayley, but my words are getting jumbled. What I'm saying doesn't sound reasonable even to me. It sounds weak and silly — like I'm trying to build a case on air.

"Hayley could explain it better," I finally say. "I can call her and see if she can come down. I know she'll want to help."

"Hayley would be the other girl involved in the thefts?" Officer Plourde asks.

"What? No! We didn't steal anything. Carrie set us up."

"She set both of you up?"

"Yes. Well, at first it was just Hayley, but somehow Carrie must have found out that I was on Hayley's side. That's when she threw *me* under the bus, too."

"Is that what made you threaten to 'expose' Ms. Freeman by coming to the police?"

"I never did that! I never said a word to her about talking to the police."

"Then how did she know you were coming here?"

"I don't know. She must have guessed it."

Plourde is looking at me like he can't quite believe I expect him to buy a word of this. I can see there's no point in saying anything else. Carrie got to him first. She put on one of her big performances and he bought it. And that's it.

"Okay," I say. "You don't believe me, I can see that. But an innocent man is in prison. So, I'm going to find a way to prove I'm telling the truth and get him out of there."

I stand up, ready to go, but Dad takes my hand and tugs me back down.

"My daughter came here to give you a statement," he says. "You may not believe what she's telling you, that's up to you, but I want you to take her statement anyway and put it on file."

Officer Plourde looks annoyed. "Our time is not to be wasted on teenage squabbles," he tells my father.

"This isn't a squabble," Dad answers. "Shana has just told you that she gave false testimony. You can look into that or you can take the other girl's word for what happened. But my daughter is trying to do the right thing, and I want it on record."

Plourde shrugs. "Suit yourself. But you should know that this could cause a lot of unnecessary trouble for your daughter."

"My daughter," Dad answers, "is telling the *truth*, as I'm sure you'll discover when you investigate the matter."

Half an hour later I've signed a statement and we're on our way back home.

"Thanks, Dad, for coming with me," I say. I want to tell him thanks for believing me, and for standing up for me, too, but I'm too close to tears to risk saying anything else.

CHAPTER SEVENTEEN

Hayley and I are eating lunch the next day when Jen comes over to our table. For a few seconds my hopes rise. I think she's there to join us. That idea is crushed when she makes no move to sit down.

"These didn't belong to any of us, so I guess they're yours," she says to me. She reaches a fist out and opens it over a bare spot on the table. A delicate gold chain and matching anklet land in a tiny heap. I recognize them as mine, although I hadn't even realized they were missing until this moment.

"It looks like she was taking things from you too, Shana," Jen says. "I don't know why you're on her side."

"Come on, Jen," I say. "You've known Hayley for a long time. Do you *really* think she'd steal anything — from anyone?"

A shadow of doubt passes over Jen's face, but I can see she's afraid to think about it too much. It's easier and safer to go along with the others, especially when one of them is Carrie. Funny that I never understood before how much power she has over the group. How long has it been this way?

I could never have admitted it until now, but there was always a thread of fear running through my friendship with Carrie. I'd seen her in action enough times to know how dirty she could get when someone crossed her. And even though we were best friends, I think I always knew that, under the right circumstances, she could turn on me, too.

Hayley gives me a sad smile after Jen has moved off. I'm sure she's sifting through as many feelings as I am as we eat lunch. It feels like everyone in the cafeteria is staring at us and it doesn't take much brainpower to figure out why. I have no doubt that Carrie is hard at work spreading stories about Hayley and me. I'm sure there is hardly a person left at the school who hasn't heard something horrible about us. And if I know Carrie, she won't have limited herself to the lies about us stealing. Whatever stories she's telling will be bigger and darker and uglier than that.

I shake my head, like that might clear away the unpleasant thoughts. There's no point in obsessing over something I can't change — at least, not right now.

"She won't be happy until she destroys us, you know," Hayley says.

It's like she's been reading my mind. "We have to find a way to prove that we're the ones telling the truth," I say.

"How?"

"I don't know," I admit. Then I remember something my mom has told me a few times. "But everyone makes mistakes when they commit crimes. That's how they get caught."

"What about the people who get away with things?" Hayley asks. Not exactly encouraging, but it's a fair question.

"I still think they all probably made mistakes," I say, "only maybe no one looked hard enough to find them."

"So, what mistake do you think Carrie made?" she asks.

"I don't know — yet. But I'm sure there's something, and all we have to do is figure it out."

"And then *prove* it," Hayley adds.

"Yes, then prove it," I agree.

"That's probably going to be the hard part," she says with a sigh.

That evening we get together at my place and write down everything that's happened so far. We write in third person, so there won't be any confusion in case we eventually have to give it to someone else to read — like the police. We organize everything by timeline. In the end, this is what we have to work with:

Facts in the Case

1. Last summer: Carrie tells Hayley she can easily get rid of the boarder she doesn't like by accusing him of molesting her.

2. Last fall: Carrie's mom and Joe Kelward (who have been dating for about a year) get engaged and then married. Carrie makes no secret of the fact that she doesn't like him and doesn't want him in her life.

3. January: Carrie accuses her new stepfather of molesting her. He is arrested and charged.

4. It's hard to know exactly when Carrie begins to worry about Hayley, but it probably wasn't long after the charges were laid against Joe. Carrie must wonder if Hayley will suspect that she made up the accusation, just as she suggested Hayley do with the boarder.

5. February: Carrie tells Shana there isn't enough evidence against Joe and she is terrified he will get off. She convinces Shana to help her by giving false testimony.

6. For several months before the trial, some of our friends begin to notice items of jewellery are missing. We learn later that Carrie is framing Hayley. We now know she did that to get rid of Hayley, so that if Hayley had any suspicions, she couldn't share them with the rest of us.

7. The trial is held and Joe is convicted. Hayley cannot hide her feelings — which is when Carrie realizes for sure that Hayley suspects that Carrie made up the story about Joe in order to get rid of him.

8. Carrie sets up the scene at Shana's house where Hayley is "caught" stealing.

9. Carrie pretends she's going to see Hayley to work things out, but actually makes up nasty messages for both Hayley and the rest of us to make sure we stop being friends.

10. Shana goes to see Hayley, learns the truth. Somehow (HOW?) Carrie finds out that Shana has taken Hayley's side.

11. Shana finds the stolen jewellery in Carrie's house, and tries to "discover" it with the others there. This backfires because Carrie has found out what she's up to and turns it all against Shana instead. (How did Carrie find out? Perhaps there's a clue there.)

12. Carrie goes to the police and tells them that Shana has threatened to recant testimony

as a way of hurting Carrie. As a result, the police do not believe Shana when she goes there to admit she lied.

"Well, that's it, I guess," I say, looking the list over. I keep staring at items ten and eleven, and I wonder out loud how Carrie found out about those things.

"It's probably something simple," Hayley says, "like she called your place and your mom told her where you'd gone, or maybe someone saw you and mentioned it to her."

"Maybe," I say.

"You can't start getting spooked about this," Hayley says. "I mean, she's just a kid, like us. She doesn't have superhuman powers or anything. It's easy to get nervous with Carrie, because she doesn't play fair, but anything she does has a normal explanation. We have to remember that."

"You're right," I say. I'm glad, really glad, that Hayley and I are on the same side.

I make a copy of our list for Hayley on my scanner. That way, we can each add notes if we think of anything else, or come up with ideas on how to expose Carrie for the lying manipulator she is.

But I have to admit, it looks kind of hopeless at this point.

CHAPTER EIGHTEEN

Besides giving myself a headache thinking about all of this, nothing has happened over the last few days. Until earlier today, that is.

I'd just dropped off resumes at a few stores in the Halifax Shopping Centre. Summer's coming soon and I'll be sixteen in July, so I'm looking forward to getting my first real job.

So, anyway, I was making the rounds in the food court on the upper level when I saw Carrie heading toward me. I don't know if she'd already seen me. She looked startled when she got close and glanced in my direction, but that could have been an act. *Everything* with Carrie is an act.

She was alone, and as soon as she saw me she made a beeline in my direction. I stood my ground, chin up, and waited while she walked right up to me.

"I guess you know by now that you made a big mistake when you decided to cross me," she said.

"I made a big mistake when I decided to be *friends* with you," I answered. I should have left it there. I should have let it go and walked away. But there was so much anger in me! It had been building for days, which is why I couldn't help but add, "You shouldn't think that you're going to get away with any of this."

She laughed at that, but it was ice cold and humourless.

"I'm so much smarter than you that I actually pity you," she said with a snort. "Like last year, when you and Mike broke up."

"What do you mean?" I asked, startled by the change of subject.

"I did that," she told me. "And you never even suspected."

I stared at her, uncomprehending, while she continued. "When I went to use your laptop that day, Mike's Facebook page was still up. He hadn't remembered to log out. So I changed his status — it took two seconds. A few minutes later when I was in my own account, I showed you his status change and you went right to pieces. It was so easy — because you're so dumb."

"Why would you have done that? We were friends then," I said, not quite believing her.

"To amuse myself, mostly. But it was annoying — you were always busy with him, or talking about him or whatever. So, I got rid of him."

I felt sick. I remembered how upset Mike had looked at school the next day. Even through my pain I'd found that odd, since he was the one who'd broken up with me. Suddenly, it made sense. I realized how cleverly Carrie had fooled both of us into thinking we'd been dumped. On Facebook, for everyone to see. What could have been more hurtful and humiliating? And that's why it had worked just as she'd planned. Neither of us had ever even tried to talk about it — our pride wouldn't let us. My heart was breaking all over again, but I forced myself not to react. "This situation isn't the same as that, Carrie. You're not going to get away with what you've done this time. I'm going to see to it."

"Oh, really. Then I see you haven't learned your lesson yet," she said. Her voice was hard, the words clipped and sharp. "I'll just have to do something about that, won't I?"

"Do whatever you want," I said. "I'm not afraid of you."

She laughed again, tossing her head back for effect. Then she walked away.

My stomach was queasy from the encounter so I decided to forget about taking around any more resumes just then. I headed to the bus stop and a few minutes later I was on my way home, which is where I am now.

There's no one here, so I decide to call Hayley to see if she wants to come over. She's not home, and there's no answer on her cell. I flop across my bed. Then I sit straight up, struck by an idea.

Carrie is at the mall. Which means she's not home right now. But chances are good that her mother is at their house and it has just occurred to me that she might be the person I need to talk to. If I can convince her of the truth, maybe she can find a way to force Carrie to admit what she did, and free Mr. Kelward.

In a flash, I'm out the door and on my way to her place. I'm breathless and my heart is thumping madly in my chest by the time I get there. I don't even wait to get my breath back before I jab my finger at the doorbell.

Carrie's mom appears at the door a moment later. She looks puzzled, and not exactly happy to see me.

"Mrs. Freeman," I say. "I need to talk to you for a few minutes."

She sighs heavily, shaking her head. "Carrie told me you might show up here one of these days, Shana," she says. "I really think you should just turn around and go home. We've been through a lot, and I'd appreciate it if you didn't try to cause any trouble."

"I don't know what she told you," I say, "but I want you to know the truth. I lied. I lied to the police and I lied in court. I never saw your husband do anything, and I believe

Carrie made the whole story up just to get rid of him."

"I asked you not to bother us," she says quietly. "Please, just go away."

Mrs. Freeman looks like she's about to cry, and I feel sorry for causing that. She reaches for the door, but I feel I need to make one last effort.

"Your husband didn't do anything wrong," I say, raising my voice so she can hear even as the door swings closed. "He's innocent! He doesn't deserve to be locked up and you don't deserve to be going through all of this. Please, believe me!"

Do I imagine it — the slight hesitation just before the final little push that closes the door completely? I stand there with the *click* of the lock echoing in my head and I'm overwhelmed with pity for the woman on the other side of the door.

I wonder if there's any doubt in her at all. Can she let herself think that her own daughter is so evil that she was willing to destroy a man's life, not to mention her own mother's happiness? And for what? Because she didn't happen to like him? Because she didn't want to give up some of her mother's attention?

I walk away, feeling worse than ever, wishing I hadn't come. What good did it do? What if Mrs. Freeman had let me in and listened to me? What if she *had* believed me? Her husband is still in prison. Even if he got out tomorrow, he'd still know that she took Carrie's side against him. How could their marriage ever be put back together again after all the terrible things that have happened?

As I head back toward home, I realize how impossible the situation is. Carrie's mom almost *has* to believe her daughter. If she lets herself think Carrie lied, her whole world will crumble even more than it already has.

It's all so hopeless and horrible.

CHAPTER NINETEEN

Mom and Dad have just gotten home. They're unpacking groceries in the kitchen and I can hear them talking in hushed tones. That doesn't necessarily mean they're talking about me, but it's definitely a conversation they don't want me to hear.

Neither of them has said anything harsh about what I did, at least not yet. That doesn't stop me from feeling guilty and a bit nervous. They have to be disappointed that I'd do something so obviously wrong. I almost wish they'd speak up and tell me how they feel and get it out in the open.

I head to the kitchen and offer to help put stuff away. Mom's smile is tight as she passes me some green bags full of canned soup and vegetables. I'm stacking them on shelves when there's a knock at the front door.

"Get that, would you Shana?" Dad says.

When I open the door I find two police officers standing there. One of them is a woman and the other is Officer Plourde. My spirits lift to think maybe he's going to take me seriously after all. But that's not what he's here for.

"Shana Tremain?" he asks, though he should know perfectly well who I am, since I talked to him just yesterday.

"Yes."

"Do you have a parent present?"

"They're in the kitchen," I say.

"We're going to ask you to accompany us to the police station to answer a few questions," Officer Plourde says. "You'll need to have a parent come with you."

A flush of heat rushes through my body. I know it's adrenaline and that it's the response to the sudden fear I'm feeling. In an instant, I'm absolutely certain that Carrie has done something else to make trouble for me.

My voice trembles as I call out for my mom and dad. They appear at the end of the hall at once and hurry toward the door as soon as they see the police standing there.

"Officers," my mom says with a nod. "Can we help you?"

"We've had some complaints that we need to investigate," the female officer says. "Can one of you bring Shana to the police station? We'd appreciate it if she'd come in to answer some questions voluntarily."

"What kind of questions?" Mom asks.

"Questions in response to a complaint we've received," Plourde answers gruffly.

Mom and Dad both look at me questioningly. I shrug, to show them I have no idea what this could be about, even though I have no doubt that Carrie is behind it.

———

Fifteen minutes later, Mom and I are pulling up to the police station. I can't help but think this particular red brick building is becoming just a little too familiar to me.

We go in, but there's no waiting this time. We're escorted into a room and a moment later the female cop comes in. She introduces herself as Officer Cloud and passes me a business card, which I stick in my pocket. Officer Cloud says that Officer Plourde will be along in just a few minutes and perhaps we can go ahead and get started without him. That's fine with me.

"Is Shana under arrest?" Mom asks.

"No. She hasn't been charged with anything at this point," Officer Cloud tells her.

"So, we're free to go anytime we want to?"

"For now, yes. Naturally, we'd encourage her to help clear this matter up."

Mom seems to think this over. Officer Cloud and I both wait silently until Mom nods and tells her she can go ahead.

"Can you tell me where you were this afternoon?" she asks, turning to me.

"I went to the shopping centre to take around some resumes," I say.

"Shana is turning sixteen soon, so she's eager to get her first job," Mom adds. Officer Cloud gives her a polite smile before addressing me again.

"And did you see anyone you knew while you were there?" she wants to know.

"I saw Carrie Freeman," I say.

"Were you speaking with Ms. Freeman?"

"For a few minutes."

"During that conversation, did you make any threatening comments toward Ms. Freeman?"

"What? No! Of course not."

"You didn't tell her you were going to see her dead?"

"No! That's crazy!"

"Or that you were going to burn her house down with her and her mother in it?"

Mom gasps at that. "Shana would never say anything like that," she says. Officer Cloud doesn't even act like she's heard her.

"I didn't say those things," I say. "As far as I'm concerned, I want nothing to do with Carrie, ever again."

"In that case, you would have had no reason to go to her house after you left the shopping centre, would you?" Officer Cloud says. Her voice is smooth, almost friendly.

"Well, I … it wasn't like you think," I say.

Mom stares at me. "Were you at Carrie's house this afternoon?" she asks.

"I wanted to tell Mrs. Freeman the truth — that her husband didn't do anything," I say. "And I knew Carrie wasn't there, so I thought it was a good time to go. Only, she didn't want to talk to me."

Officer Cloud makes a few notes. She asks me if I'd sign a statement, but Mom says I'm not signing anything. She says this whole thing has gotten out of hand and that I won't be answering anymore questions unless I have a lawyer present. Then she tells me we're leaving. I'm shaking on the way out. It feel as though someone is going to come running after us any second and have me arrested. But no one tries to stop us and we make it to the car and drive home.

Mom tells Dad that she doesn't feel like cooking so we order in a pizza and salad. When the delivery guy knocks I nearly jump out of my skin, I'm so on edge. I nibble a bit of salad and manage to swallow a few bites of pizza before giving up.

I call Hayley later and tell her about the whole thing.

"We need to be super careful," she says. "Honestly, it might be a good idea to stick together when we go anywhere for a while."

"We can't let Carrie win that way," I protest. Even so, I know she's right. It's hard to fight lies when you can't prove that's what they are.

After we hang up, I get out my list of what's happened to add today's events to it. And that's when I notice something that might help!

CHAPTER TWENTY

I stare at the two points on the list for a moment. Numbers eleven and twelve:

11. Shana finds stolen jewellery in Carrie's house, and tries to "discover" it with the others there. This backfires as Carrie has found out what she's up to and turns it all against Shana instead. (How did Carrie find out? Perhaps there's a clue there.)

12. Carrie goes to the police and tells them that Shana has threatened to recant testimony as a way of hurting Carrie. As a result, the police do not believe Shana when she goes there to admit she lied.

It has just occurred to me that these two things may, in fact, be listed backwards. The big blow-up at Carrie's place happened on Saturday. I went to the police the next day and I'm almost positive that Officer Plourde told me that Carrie had been in a few days before then. That means she went to them *before* the showdown at her place on Saturday.

It's not much, but it's something. If only someone will listen to me!

I pick up my cellphone and dig the card Officer Cloud gave me out of my pocket. She's still on duty, but not at the station, and someone promises they'll have her call me back as soon as she can.

That turns out to be less than ten minutes.

"Do you have the file there in front of you?" I ask.

"Do I need it?" she asks. She sounds tired and impatient.

"I think so. I think there's something in there that will prove Carrie is lying."

"Hang on," she says. I hear muffled voices in the background, the sound of a chair scraping on the floor, footsteps, and some paper shuffling. Then there's a thud, the kind that's made by a book or stack of paper landing on a flat surface.

"Okay, so what've you got?" Officer Cloud asks, coming back on the line.

"The date that Carrie went there and said I had told her I was going to try to make trouble for her."

"What about it?"

I explain how I found the stolen items at Carrie's place. "She must have realized it, though. So she set me up for when the others were around — which she couldn't possibly have done if we'd already had a fight about it."

"And?" says Officer Cloud.

"The big blow-up with her happened on Saturday. And there are three other girls who were there, so they're witnesses to that. The thing about it is that that it happened *after* she made that statement to Officer Plourde about the thefts. That *proves* she lied."

There's silence for a few seconds — just enough time for me to picture her rolling her eyes or sighing. But then she asks me for the names and contact information for the other girls.

I give her the details, but I can't help wondering if Carrie has thought of this, too. If she has, she'll have done her best to find a way around it. When I think of how she convinced me to lie — in court — I can't help but wonder if she could have persuaded the others to lie about Saturday. She's perfectly capable of coming up with a story that would make that seem reasonable to them. The web of lies could be endless.

"Is there anything else?" Officer Cloud asks after she's written down names and phone numbers for Lori, Jen, and Krysti.

"No. That's it."

She says she'll look into it, but she doesn't sound too excited about it. After we hang up I sit and wonder what good it's going to do even if she does ask the others. It doesn't establish that Carrie lied about her stepfather, and that's the thing I really need to be able to prove.

For a moment I can picture his face, smiling and friendly, when he first became Carrie's stepdad. I hadn't been able to understand why she didn't like him back then. He seemed genuinely nice to me. It had seemed to make sense when she told me he'd been molesting her, but now I know that was a lie. What was it, then, that made her dislike him? Could anyone really be so selfish and evil that they would do what she did for no reason other than she didn't happen to want him around? Didn't she even care what that did to her *mother*?

But the image of Joe Kelward's smiling face fades and gives way to a different expression. I see, instead, the hard, angry look that stared back at me when I was on the witness stand. I recall seeing panic in his eyes, and how that gave me a feeling of satisfaction at the time, thinking he was getting what he deserved.

Except he wasn't.

Nausea washes over me and I have to take long, slow breaths to settle it. My shoulders slump forward as tears fill my eyes and spill over. How could I have gotten myself into such a terrible predicament? Why couldn't I have just said no to Carrie in the first place? I knew what I was doing was wrong, even if it *seemed* like it was for a good reason at the time.

Glancing around my room I can't help wondering what it's like where Joe Kelward is right now. I picture a small cell with a narrow bed sporting a thin mattress. There would be a sink and toilet right there in the same room, and zero privacy for when he wanted to use them. This innocent man has to eat and shower and spend his days with murderers and rapists and other criminals.

I can't begin to imagine the despair he feels. Knowing that it's at least partly my fault is like a burden that gets heavier with each passing day. If only there was something I could do to help him.

That's when it occurs to me that maybe there is something I can do. It might not be much, but I can write to him. I can tell him what happened and let him know I'm doing what I can to try to right the wrong that's been done to him.

I can give him hope.

CHAPTER TWENTY-ONE

The letter to Joe Kelward is hard to write, but I get it done. It's not until I have it in an envelope and sealed that I realize I have no idea where to send it. There are lots of prisons across the country and he could be in any one of them as far as I know.

I text Hayley to see if she has any ideas on how to find him. Good thing, because she comes up with something and texts back: "Maybe his lawyer?" right away.

Of course! His lawyer would know where he'd been sent. And that produces another idea. The lawyer might be able to give me some advice on other things I can do to help get Kelward out of jail. Even though I can't do anything until tomorrow, it gives me the most hope I've felt in the past week.

I type a few words into a search engine and find his lawyer's name, along with three others in the law firm of Coulter, Leland, Hatton, and Stone. After jotting down the phone number and address, I crawl into bed.

I sleep a little better than I have in the past few nights.

Monday at lunch is the first chance I have to call the lawyer. The secretary who answers the phone is startlingly cheery. I blurt out a request to speak to Mr. Hatton.

"I'm sorry, but Mr. Hatton isn't in at the moment. Would you like to go to his voice mail?"

"Uh, can I leave him a message?" I ask. Then I realize that's exactly what she just said to me.

"Certainly," she says smoothly, as if she hadn't suggested it one second ago. "I'll put you through."

A female voice announces that I've reached the voice mail of Aaron Hatton and promises that he'll get back to me as soon as he can.

'Hi," I say. And the rest comes out in a rush. "I testified against your client, Joe Kelward, but it was a mistake and I feel terrible about it and I want to help him. I already went to the police only she got there first — Carrie, I mean, and I think they believed her instead of me even though I'm the one telling the truth. Also, I have a letter I want to send to him, but I don't know where he is or anything so if you could call me with his address — for the letter — and maybe give me some advice or pointers or whatever on how I can help fix this, that would be great. I don't mean legal advice. Or, I guess maybe that's what I need, only I can't pay anything."

I finish up by reciting my phone number, then repeating it, and hang up. The jumble of words I've just blurted out are echoing in my ears like so much gibberish. A monkey could have left a more sensible message. I think about calling the secretary back and asking her to erase it and let me leave a new one. But I don't bother. There's no point. I'm terrible at leaving voice mails and I know I'll do as bad or worse if I get another chance.

As I power off my phone and turn to head toward my first afternoon class, I see Krysti standing just a few feet away. Her mouth is pressed pencil-line thin and there's fury in her eyes. She stares at me for a second or two before spinning around and marching away. I can't help but feel a stab of hurt when I think that a few short days ago she was my friend. That thought is quickly chased away by the realization that Krysti is almost certainly on her way to tell Carrie what she heard. I decide not to worry about that. It's not likely Carrie will try to tell any of her lies to the lawyer who defended her stepfather.

I check my phone between classes. Hatton still hasn't called me back by the end of the afternoon. Maybe he thinks it was a prank call. Maybe he figures he has better things to do than call back some mumbling kid. I make up my mind that if he hasn't called me back by tomorrow, I'll ask my mom or dad to phone him. I know he's more likely to listen to an adult, but I can't help wanting to do this one thing on my own. In the meantime, I decide not to mention it to my folks.

The phone finally rings just past eight o'clock, but when I look at the display it's not coming from any law firm. I blink, looking at the caller's ID.

Carrie Freeman.

It's tempting to just let it ring. I have nothing to say to her, and I can't imagine that she has anything to say to me that I want to hear.

More than anything, it's curiosity that makes me press "talk" and say hello.

The first sounds I hear aren't words. It's a rasping, gasping noise that I need a few seconds to identify.

She's crying.

Then, finally, a gulp of air and, "Shana?"

"Yeah."

"Shana, I don't know what to say. I've done such terrible things and caused so much trouble, and —" Her words trail off into full sobs.

I wait, stunned into silence by what I'm

hearing. Finally, she gets herself under control and goes on.

"The worst thing of all is what I did to you," she says with a breaking voice. "To us. You were the best friend I ever had. And I don't blame you if you never forgive me, but I want you to know I'm so, so sorry. I'd do anything to prove it to you."

It's hard not to doubt her. I've seen Carrie in action too many times. But the heartbreak in her voice sounds so genuine, I can't help but hope she's telling the truth. So I ask a question that should prove whether or not she means what she's saying.

"Like go to the police and tell the truth?"

There's a pause, just a slight one. Then she says, "Yes. I'll go to the police and tell them everything."

"When?" I ask.

"Tomorrow," she promises. "There's someone else I need to talk to first."

"Your mom?"

"Yes." She breaks down crying for another minute or two, and then says, "Shana? Would you do one thing for me? Would you come over and be here with me while I tell my mom?"

I only hesitate for a second before I answer.

"I'll be right there."

CHAPTER TWENTY-TWO

Mom and Dad are watching *Jeopardy* when I head toward the door. I decide not to tell them where I'm going. That would just lead to a lot of questions and slow me down. My best friend needs me.

My best friend. In spite of everything she did, I have to admit that there's a happy flutter in my chest at the thought that it's all going to be okay. And Carrie isn't the only one who did wrong. I did, too. If I expect people to forgive me, I need to be able to forgive her, as well.

I leave a note on the kitchen table that says I've gone for a walk and I slip out the side door. My steps are light as I walk the familiar route to Carrie's house. I'm so eager to get there. Oh, I know it will be awkward for the first bit, but I'm sure that won't last.

I see her as soon as her house comes into view. She's waiting in the backyard, sitting on a big wooden swing set under a huge oak tree. How many times have we sat there, sipping soft drinks and talking about everything and anything?

As I get near, her arm comes up in a long, slow wave and she smiles nervously.

"I can't believe you came," she says. "I thought you probably hated me."

"I was upset, but now it's all going to be okay. We'll do this together — remember I'm guilty, too. And then it will be over with."

She nods solemnly and steps down off the swing. "My mom will be home soon," she says. "I'm so scared to face her. I think I might be sick."

She leans forward then, clutching her stomach. "Can you get me a bottle of water?" she asks.

I dash up the back steps, into the house and down the hall to the kitchen. A moment later I hurry back to the yard. I don't see Carrie. Maybe she made a run for the bathroom. I'm about to turn to go back inside when something hard and heavy crashes into the back of my head. It sends me sprawling forward onto the ground. The last thing that registers before everything goes black is Carrie's bottle of water rolling away from me.

The pain is so intense that at first it's the only thing I can focus on. My head is throbbing *ka-whump*, *ka-whump*, like it's about to explode.

My hand reaches up automatically and comes away wet and sticky.

I moan and register the fact that there's something in my mouth. A strip of cloth is tied around my head. And somehow, I still don't quite understand what's happened.

I breathe in slowly through my nose and try to get my bearings. Ignoring the pain, I look around. It only takes a second for me to realize I'm lying on the floor of the shed in Carrie's backyard. When I try to move, I find my ankles are tied together with a rope and fastened to the wall. In addition, my hands are bound behind me with what feels like a strip of cloth.

That's when the fear really hits me. Of course, I know Carrie hit me, but that's not going to be the end of it. The whack on the head was just the beginning of whatever it is she has planned. Terror grips me as I realize how completely I am at her mercy.

I fight to remain calm. Fumbling for my phone, I manage to extract it from my back pocket, but I quickly realize it's useless. Sure, I can call 911 but with a gag in my mouth I can't speak to tell them what's happening or where I am. Even if they follow up on the call, who knows how long it will take for them to figure out where the signal came from. I don't have the slightest doubt that it will be too late for me by then.

I struggle to remain calm and think.

And then, there she is. The shed door opens letting in light. It looks strangely like a halo behind Carrie's evil head. She smiles.

"Krysti told me about your little phone call to Joe's lawyer. Did you *really* think you could outsmart me? Or that I was just going to sit back and let you make trouble for me? I worked too hard to get rid of Joe — I wasn't about to let you ruin everything."

She moves forward ever so slightly. I see that her left hand is holding something. A jug — like the one my dad keeps gas in for the lawnmower. A rush of horror runs through me.

"Oh, I see you've noticed this," Carrie says, lifting her arm. She turns it so the wide side is angled toward me and I see a familiar, half-torn sticker. She sees the recognition on my face. She smiles.

"That's right, Shana. I got this from *your* place. That way, when you die tragically in the fire, it will prove *you're* the one who started it. They'll see that you came here to make good on the threat I reported. Except, something heavy fell and hit you on the back of the head, knocking you out while the fire you set blazed around you. And, of course, your gag and the ties around your wrists and ankles will be gone — burned away by the flames."

I see that she's wearing vinyl gloves as she unscrews the cap and tips the jug forward. Gas splashes out, the heavy smell of it filling the air in the shed.

"I don't know why you ever thought you could beat me," she says. Her voice is casual, as if she's talking about some everyday thing. "You never could lie very convincingly. I knew something was up for days before you went snooping in my closet. Didn't take much to catch you, either — not when I had some help from a special friend."

She pauses and smiles at me. "I can see you're wondering who that might have been," she says. "Remember that new teddy bear I got, just before Mom married Joe?"

I try not to react, but I'm curious and it probably shows on my face.

"It's a Nanny Cam!" she announces with a laugh. "It was supposed to catch Joe doing naughty things to me, but he wouldn't bite no matter what I did to tempt him. Luckily, I had you to help back up my story."

She laughs again and it sends a cold shiver up my back. "Turns out it was a good investment, anyway," she says. "I've gotten lots of great footage since I bought that thing, but your face when you found the jewellery — that was the best ever."

She lays the gas jug on its side on the floor, right by my head. Then she draws a book of matches from her pocket. Before she can strike one, I kick hard with my feet to get her attention. She rolls her eyes as she pauses to look at me. It's like she's wondering why I'm bothering her when she's busy trying to kill me. I lift my bound hands so she can see the cellphone I've been holding close to my side.

"So what?" she says. She's trying to sound confident but I hear the doubt in her voice. "You couldn't have made a call. And I'd have seen you typing if you'd tried to send a text."

She's right, of course. I couldn't do either of those things. She's sneering triumphantly when the sound of an incoming message bursts from her pocket.

I watch while she pulls out her phone and flips it open. If my head wasn't hurting so much, I might even have enjoyed seeing her eyes widen and her face twist in panic.

A film clip capturing everything she's said and done in the last few moments has just been sent to everyone on my Top Five list. And, of course, that list includes my "best friend," Carrie.

EPILOGUE

Four months have gone by since that day, but it won't stop playing in my memory.

As soon as Carrie realized there was no way to lie or scheme her way out of that one, she was gone in a flash. She left me lying in the shed — tied and gagged and bleeding on a gasoline-soaked floor. She headed west, hitchhiking, and made it as far as Kingston, Ontario, before being picked up by the OPP and sent back.

It was Jen who first saw the video and called the police. It couldn't have been more than a few minutes after Carrie took off when a squad car drove up with its siren blaring, but I can tell you it *felt* like an hour. An ambulance came, too, and took me to the hospital where they treated my head wound and kept me overnight.

Carrie is facing charges for a bunch of things, including what she did to Joe Kelward, and to me. Because what she did was so serious, they remanded her to the Nova Scotia Youth Facility until her trial comes up. Thankfully, Joe Kelward was freed quite quickly after the truth came out. I heard he's living somewhere in Dartmouth and putting his life back together. Alone. I never did send him that letter, but I know he's heard about everything that happened. I hope he can forgive me someday for my part in all of this. When I think about the trail of hurt and betrayal I helped create, I'm not sure I'll ever be able to completely forgive myself.

Our group of friends is back together, except things are still a bit shaky. Hayley and I are closer than we used to be, but I think Krysti still resents me, even though she now knows the truth. Jen and Lori seem a little distant. Maybe they're embarrassed for not seeing what was really going on. Maybe it will take longer for the wounds left by anger and suspicion to heal.

I no longer have a best friend. And while there are things about that which I still miss, there is something good and pure in the freedom.

And yet, I am left with a kind of sadness that I can't quite explain.

ACKNOWLEDGEMENTS

Many warm thanks to my editor, Shannon Whibbs, for her enthusiasm and insights. Also for her highly entertaining tweets.

Also by Valerie Sherrard

Accomplice
978-1554887644
$9.99

Lexie Malton is an average Vancouver teen with fairly typical issues. But she has a secret. Her ex-boyfriend, Devlin Mather, is now a heroin addict living on the street, and only Lexie knows that she's the one who put him there. Guilt makes her give in to Devlin's demands for money time and time again, even though she knows how dangerous his drug use is. Lexie finally gathers the strength to stop enabling Devlin. But when he seeks treatment for his addiction, Lexie finds herself drawn back to him, never guessing what a dark and deadly path she has just chosen.

Watcher
978-1-554884-315
$12.99

Sixteen-year-old Porter Delaney has his future figured out, but his nice, neat plans are shaken when a man he believes may be his father suddenly appears in his Toronto neighbourhood. Porter knows that he wants nothing to do with the deadbeat dad who abandoned him and his sister twelve years earlier, but curiosity causes him to re-examine the past. Unfortunately, actual memories are scarce and confusing, and much of what he knows is based on things his mother told him. As Porter looks for answers, it begins to seem that all he's ever going to find are more questions.

Three Million Acres of Flame
978-1550027273
$12.99

The year 1825 turned the lives of the Haverill family upside down. Following the death of their mother, Skye and her brother, Tavish, have adjusted to life with a single parent. And when they're asked to make another adjustment — when his father remarries and his new wife becomes pregnant — Skye finds that some changes are too much to handle. But family struggles quickly become irrelevant when the Haverills and their community are caught up in the Miramichi Fire, the largest land fire in North American history.

Speechless
978-1550027013
$12.99

When his teacher announces that it's time for the yearly class speeches, Griffin Maxwell starts to sweat. His past experience with the dreaded speech was humiliating, to say the least, and he just knows there's no way he can go through *that* again. So Griffin's best friend, Bryan, comes up with a solution — one that's so simple it just *has* to work. But neither boy can begin to predict the bizarre chain of events that will be set in place when Griffin goes along with the idea.

From squaring off with the school bully to reading a teacher's private letters, Griffin Maxwell will have to face things he never imagined, and all without saying a word!

Available at your favourite bookseller.

DUNDURN
www.dundurn.com

What did you think of this book?
Visit *www.dundurn.com*
for reviews, videos, updates, and more!